BLOOM

THE SURPRISING SEEDS
OF SORREL FALLOWFIELD

Books by Nicola Skinner

BLOOM: THE SURPRISING SEEDS OF SORREL FALLOWFIELD

STORM

But look – try not to worry. Even if you *are* infected at least you won't be the only one. It happened to us too. We *all* look a little weird here.

Or, as Mum would say diplomatically, 'Haven't we *grown*, Sorrel?'

And yes, that is my name. Mum has a thing about fresh herbs. It could have been worse, I suppose. She also loves parsley.

CHAPTER 1

WHEN THE NEWSPAPERS and journalists first got hold of my story they wrote a lot of lies. The main ones were:

1. I was the child of a broken home.

2. Mum was a terrible single mother.

3. With a background like mine, it wasn't any wonder I did what I did.

None of them was true – well, apart from Mum being a single mum. But it wasn't her fault my dad had done a runner when I was a baby. Yet one of the headlines stuck in my head. I *did* come from a broken home.

Oh, not in the way they meant it, in the 'I wore ragged trousers and brushed my teeth with sugar' sort of way. But our house did feel worn out and broken down – something was always going wrong.

If you'd ever popped in, you'd have felt it too.

The tick of the clock in the hallway would follow you around the house like it was tutting at you. The tap in the kitchen would go *drip, drip, drip* as if it was crying about something. If you sat down in front of the telly, it would lose sound halfway through whatever was on, as if it had gone into a monumental sulk and wasn't speaking to anyone *ever* again. *Ever.*

There was a ring of black mould round the whole bath, our curtains were constantly pinging off their rods in some desperate escape mission and every time we flushed the loo the pipes would moan and groan at what we'd made them swallow. Oh yes, if you visited our house, you'd want to leave within seconds. You'd garble out an excuse, like: 'Er, just remembered . . . I promised Mum I was going to hoover the roof today! Gotta go!' And you'd get away as fast as you could.

Apart from my best friend Neena, not many people stayed long at our home.

And guess what it was called?

Cheery Cottage.

To be honest, though, I didn't blame anyone that ran away. Because it wasn't *just* the damp and the taps and the protesting pipes. It was more than all of that.

It was the feeling in the house. And it was everywhere.

A gloomy glumness. A grumpy grimness. A grimy greyness. Cheery Cottage always felt cross and unhappy about something, and there was almost nothing this mood didn't infect. It inched into everything, from the saggy sofa in the lounge, to the droopy fake fern in the hallway, which always looked as if it was dying of thirst, even though *it was plastic*.

And – worst of all – this misery sometimes seeped into Mum too. Oh, she'd never say as much, but I'd know. It was in her when she sat at the kitchen table, staring into space. It was in her when she shuffled downstairs in the mornings. I'd look at her. She'd look at me. And in the scary few seconds before she finally smiled, I'd think: *It's spreading.*

But what could *I* do to fix things? I wasn't a plumber. I was the shortest kid in our year, so I couldn't reach the curtain poles. When it came to fixing the telly, all I knew was the old Whack and Pray method.

Instead, I had a different solution. And it was to follow this very simple rule:

Be good at school and be good at home, and do what I was told in both.

So, that's what I did.

I was good at being good.

I was so good, Mum regularly ran out of shoeboxes in which to put my Sensible Child and School Rule Champion certificates.

I was so good, trainee teachers came to *me* to clear up any questions they had about Grittysnit School rules. Like:

Are pupils allowed to sprint outside?

(Answer: never. A slight jog is allowed if you are in danger – for example, if you are being chased by a bear – and even then, you must obtain written permission twenty-eight days in advance.)

Are you allowed to smile at Mr Grittysnit, our headmaster?

(Answer: never. He prefers a lowered gaze as a mark of respect.)

Has he always been so strict and scary?

(Answer: technically, this is not a question about school rules, but seeing as you're new, I will let you off, just this once. And yes.)

I was so good, I was Head of Year for the second year running.

I was so good, my nickname at school was Good Girl Sorrel. Well, it *had* been Good Girl Sorrel, until sometime around the beginning of Year Five when Chrissie Valentini had changed it *ever so slightly* to 'Suck-up Sorrel'. But I never told the teachers.

That's how good I was.

And every time I came home from school with the latest proof, Mum would smile and call me her Good Girl. And that broken feeling would leave her and sneak back into the corners of the house.

For a while.

CHAPTER 2

AND THEN, ON the first day of Year Six last September, something else broke too. Something I was quite fond of. My life.

It was the patio's fault.

I'd let myself in from school. Mum was still working, the lucky thing, at The Best Job In The World, and wouldn't get back for another two and a half hours. I planned to unwind by cleaning the kitchen, polishing my school shoes and doing my homework, because that was how I rolled.

Now, Mum wasn't a big fan of me being home alone, but she worked full-time every day and didn't get back till 5.45 p.m. We could only afford three days of After-school Club: Wednesdays, Thursdays and Fridays. On Tuesdays, I went to Neena's house after school. (Who, for a while, depending on which news programme was on, was either my gormless best friend, evil partner in crime, evil best friend or gormless partner in crime.)

Anyway, Mondays were my home-alone afternoons. On Monday mornings, Mum would *always* say: 'Don't burn the house down, and make sure you do your homework.' As if I needed telling. Who knew exactly what she should be doing at any given time? Who had written Sorrel's Stupendous Schedule?

I had, that's who. My Stupendous Schedule played a big part in my being good. It's *sooo* much easier to toe the line when you have a row of neat little boxes waiting to be ticked.

So there I was. Wiping sticky marmalade patches off our table. Emptying the dishwasher. Opening the back door to air the kitchen, which always smelled damp.

Once I'd done all that, it was 4.25 p.m. I had just a few more precious moments of leisure time before I had to crack on with my homework, and I knew exactly how to spend them.

I went to my rucksack and took out the letter which had been given to us at the end of school that very day. And this time, I didn't skim it, surrounded by noisy classmates. I devoured every single word.

This is what it said:

Are the buttons always shiny on your blazer?

Do you regularly come home with Perfect
Behaviour reports?
Could YOU be the winner of the school
competition to find the Grittysnit Star of
the Year?
There's only one way to find out.

Enter my **GRITTYSNIT STAR** competition
for the chance to be crowned THE MOST
AMAZING **GRITTYSNIT STAR** OF THE ENTIRE
SCHOOL AND LITTLE STERILIS at the end
of term.

You will also win a seven-day family holiday in the
Lotsa Rays Holiday Resort in Portugal. (Prize kindly
donated by local travel agency Breakz Away.)

A family holiday in the sun! I'd never been abroad
before, let alone on a plane. Mum always said money
was a bit too tight for that. As if our money was an
uncomfortable jumper.

On the letter, someone – probably the school
secretary, Mrs Pinch – had drawn four little matchstick
figures sunbathing on a beach. They were holding
ice-cream cones and smiling at each other.

They looked happy.

I read on.

The winning GRITTYSNIT STAR will possess that special something that makes an ideal Grittysnit child.

I held my breath. *What?*

Each child will be judged on their ability to obey the school rules every second of the day.

I gasped in delight. That was me!

I did a quick mental calculation. There were sixty children in each year at Grittysnits. I'd be up against 419 other entrants. Or would I? I had six full years' practice of obeying school rules. The odds were in my favour. Most kids in Reception and the early years could barely tie their own shoelaces, let alone mind their pees and, for that matter, their queues.

Winning that holiday would be like taking candy from a baby. I almost felt guilty as I mentally marked the number of competitors down. *Them's the breaks, kids.*

The most important thing to remember is that
the Grittysnit Star will be a living embodiment
of our school motto, BLINKIMUS BLONKIMUS
FUDGEYMUS LATINMUS. Or, in English . . .

I didn't even have to read the English translation,
I knew it so well. Looking up for a moment, I caught
sight of my reflection in the kitchen window. Standing
solemnly in front of me was a short, round, pale and
freckly girl, her hair (the washed-out yellow of mild
Cheddar) scraped back in a bun. She returned my gaze
confidently, as if to say, 'School motto? Cut me and I
bleed school motto.'

Together, we chanted: 'May obedience shape you.
May conformity mould you. May rules polish you.'

The tap dripped sadly.

I read on.

The lucky winner will also enjoy other
special privileges. These will include:

1. Having your own chair on the staff stage
during school assemblies.
2. Never having to queue for lunch.

3. A massive badge (in regulation grey) which says:

I AM THE
MOST
OBEDIENT
CHILD
IN THIS
ENTIRE SCHOOL.

What, you want more? That's the problem with children these days — it's all take, take, take.

May the best child win.
Now, go and do your homework.

Your headmaster,
Mr Grittysnit

I put the letter down and took a big shaky breath. This was my *destiny*. Window girl and I looked solemnly at each other, as if bound by a silent pact.

Holding the letter as gently as if it was made of glass, I walked over to the fridge. I wanted to fix it there with a magnet so I could see it every day. But finding a space would not be easy. Already the fridge was plastered with yellowing bills, old recipes Mum tore out of magazines . . .

And, of course, that photo of us on our most recent summer holiday, taken just a fortnight before. It showed us on a small pebbly beach, huddled under a blanket, beneath a sky as grey as the bags under Mum's eyes.

I stared at that photo, remembering. How the caravan had smelled of somebody else's life that we'd wandered into by mistake. How Mum had spent the whole week begging me not to break anything. How it had rained for six days straight and then, just as we'd boarded the coach back to Little Sterilis, the sun had come out.

Which had made everything worse somehow.

Mum had spent the whole journey back – all five hours of it – with her forehead squished up against the window, staring at the blue sky like it was someone else's birthday cake and she knew she wouldn't get a slice.

Next to the photo was our calendar for the year ahead. I saw that Mum had marked our summer holidays on it *already*. CARAVAN, she'd written, in thick red ink. No exclamation marks. No smiley faces.

To be honest, it looked more like a threat than a holiday.

But if I won the Grittysnit Star competition, we could have a proper family holiday, somewhere sunny. Somewhere *else*. My yearning hardened into determination. All I had to do was be perfect for the next eight weeks.

No sweat.

I'd just fixed Mr Grittysnit's letter over the photo, feeling immense relief as Mum's troubled frown disappeared, when . . .

SLAM! The back door whipped open with a bang.

My heart hammered with fright. *Who's there?*

But it was no one. Just a gust of wind and a door nearly swinging off its hinges. I must not have shut it properly after airing the kitchen earlier.

The wind roared in and seemed to fill the entire kitchen with anger. I felt as if I was standing in a room of invisible fury. On legs as wobbly as cooked spaghetti, I staggered over to shut the door and force the wind out.

Something white and fluttery flew over my shoulder. I shrieked and ducked down.

Is a pigeon trapped in our kitchen?

I looked closer. It wasn't a white pigeon, all claws and feathers. It was Mr Grittysnit's letter! The wind had ripped it off the fridge and it was flying frantically about the room. When I jumped up to catch it, it darted out of reach, as if invisible blustery hands had snatched it away. I just caught a glimpse of the stick figures hovering in mid-air, their smiles turned to frozen grimaces, before they flapped and fluttered . . .

. . . out of the doorway and into our backyard.

CHAPTER 3

I *WANTED THAT* letter. It would spur me on, a promise of better days. I took a deep breath and followed it outside.

I did a quick scan of the patio. It didn't take long. Everything seemed the same. The two plastic chairs we never sat in. Weeds pushing up between the concrete paving slabs. And the tall weeping willow tree, right at the back, casting its shadow over our house.

I'd have been weeping too if I looked like that.

Its grey trunk was smothered in bright red hairy growths that looked like boils. Its branches dragged on the concrete as if it was hanging its head in misery. Even its leaves were ugly – black and withered and lifeless. Really, the tree didn't so much grow as squat at the end of our garden, like a dying troll with a skin condition. Mum said it was diseased. I'd say.

And there was no sign of Mr Grittysnit's letter. I was about to give it up for lost when a fluttering movement at the base of the tree caught my eye. It had somehow got wrapped round one of the tree's withered branches. I could just about make out the words *Each child will be judged* and one stick figure pinned underneath a bunch of shrivelled leaves. I felt sorry for it. This wasn't the holiday of a lifetime, lying under a septic tree in a damp backyard.

'I'll take that, thank you very much.' I lifted up the branch gingerly – reluctant to catch its disease, whatever it was – and bent down to pick up the letter.

ZING! The air took on an electric charge and vibrated with a terrible force. The sounds in the garden became exaggerated with a horrid loudness. The rustling dead leaves in the branches above me were a booming rattle. A pigeon cooed and it sounded like a chainsaw. But more frightening than all of that were the gaps of silence between the sounds. They were eerie and powerful and strong.

It felt—

I'VE BEEN WAITING FOR YOU.

I spun on my heels. *Who said that?*

My heart thumped so loudly I could barely hear anything. Yet the patio was empty.

Icy sweat drenched my skin. Everything was real

and unreal, too loud and too quiet at once.

Come on, Sorrel, breathe in and out, nice and slow. I calmed down enough to try to think. What had just happened? I'd only bent down to pick up the letter. Had the tree poisoned me, sent a hideous disease to my brain which had caused me to start hearing things? Or perhaps I'd had a rush of blood to the head when I'd bent down? Maybe I hadn't had enough to eat. Maybe I should go into the kitchen and investigate the snack situation.

But what is that, moving near my feet? Rats?

There it was again!

But as I peered around me, shaking with fear, I realised there wasn't anything black and wriggly next to my feet.

The movement had come from *under* my feet.

As if there was a . . . thing. Underneath the concrete.

Turning over.

Down there.

'Hello?'

I sounded like a baby lamb bleating alone on a hill.

'Is anyone there?'

The windows in the house gave me blank stares.

RUN, I told myself. NOW!

I managed one step away from the tree when the patio slab under my feet moved up and down, as if something deep down in the earth was trying to *shake* the concrete – or me – off itself.

Is this an earthquake?

My mouth opened to scream but no sound came out. Gasping, I looked down again. Like a twig snapping, the slab under my feet cracked clean in two. The crack gained momentum, ripping its way through the patio all the way from the tree to the back door. It broke the patio as easily as a warm knife slicing through butter, leaving behind a trail of smashed concrete.

The damage was worst by the tree. The concrete round its trunk had shattered outwards in a crude circle of fractured slabs. It looked like it was trying to smile through a mouthful of broken teeth. I saw something, stuck in the cracked slab under my feet.

And I couldn't look away.

CHAPTER 4

You know when you go Easter egg hunting and you have a hunch where an egg is going to be right before you find it in that very spot? I had that feeling. Like someone had put a little treasure down there for me to find.

Not only that, but it had been there my whole life. Waiting for me.

I felt exhausted and terrified, as wrung out as an old sock stuck in a spin cycle for too long. Yet I sank to my knees and peered closer. The thing in the slab was brown and papery. I could only see the top of it, but it looked like a leaf.

And here was the weird thing. Even though the sensible part of me was jumping up and down with disbelief – what was I doing, trying to rescue a random leaf, when I should be inside, running for cover before another earthquake? – there was another part of me with different ideas. And it seemed to be winning the battle of wills, because there I was, sweaty and hot and obsessed with jabbing my fingers into a broken concrete lump so I could pull this thing out.

Then it glowed.

I stared at it. I rubbed my eyes. Engaged the old eyeballs again. But no – it was not glowing now. Yet for a second it had looked almost alive . . .

All of a sudden, I didn't care about my homework. I didn't care about my schedule. I didn't even care about my school trousers getting dirty. I eagerly reached down. But my fingers were too wide and it was wedged at least fifteen centimetres too deep. My fingertips scrabbled desperately but touched only air.

I ran into the kitchen, yanked open a kitchen drawer and rummaged around with shaking hands. What I needed was something narrow and sharp to stick down the crack and fish out what was down there. Barbecue tongs? No, they wouldn't fit in the gap. A cocktail stick? That could work!

I ran back outside, kneeled down on the paving slab and poked the cocktail stick down the gap. It fitted perfectly but wasn't long enough. I could have cried with frustration. I didn't know why it mattered so much. I was spellbound somehow.

I hurried inside, pulled open the second kitchen drawer and found a yellowing plastic wallet stuffed with paperwork and a roll of cling film. Great if you wanted to cling-film some paperwork; less great if you wanted to impale something inexplicable your patio had just thrown up.

Forget your little rescue mission. Just get back to your schedule and make up for lost time.

I went to retrieve Mr Grittysnit's letter from underneath the willow tree and threw a final glance at the cracked paving slab. That was weird. The thing stuck down there seemed to have . . . moved.

I could see a brown corner poking out now. That would make it much easier to pull out. But hadn't it been wedged so far down my fingers hadn't been able to touch it?

At that point, I could have done the sensible thing. Walked back into the house and called the emergency services. Reported an Unidentified Brown Papery Thing and had it removed by the authorities. Lived off the excitement for a couple of weeks, and then got on with my life.

But I didn't.

And that is something I have to live with for the rest

of my life. And potentially, although it's *very unlikely*, so will you. But let me offer you an important bit of advice just for your peace of mind.

If you are in any way changed by this book, you may feel, at first, like blaming me. But you're going to have to push past that, seriously. Blame is a toxic emotion that will only, in the end, make *you* suffer, not me. So remember. No blame. No hate. Aim for brave acceptance instead. I offer you this advice as a friend. Or you could always try punching a pillow – apparently that helps.

Where were we? Oh yes. Shivering a little in the shadows, I looked again. I was right – the old papery object *had* moved. The top half of it now stuck out of the slab completely. *How had that happened?*

My brain leaped ahead of me, desperate to provide answers. Perhaps there was another tremor when I was in the kitchen just now and the shockwaves made it move?

I bent down and reached. As the tips of my fingers brushed the object, a jolt of energy ran all the way up my arm, like tiny electric shocks skipping up my bones. For a second, a vision flashed in my brain. Bright green grass, damp with dew. A tangle of tree roots.

I pulled the entire thing free, and straightened up. It was in my hands, so light it was almost weightless.

I stared at it eagerly, wondering what treasure I had discovered.

It was a . . .

. . . brown paper envelope.

A brown paper envelope, ladies and gentlemen.

Disappointed yet also completely mystified, I brushed the earth off it, revealing some curly writing on one side which said: *THE SURPRISING SEEDS.* The words were scrawled in faded, old-fashioned green ink.

Underneath that was the sentence *SELF-SEEDING BE THESE SEEDS.*

I turned the packet over, hoping to find more explanation, or at least something *a bit more exciting*, but there was nothing.

No instructions.

No use-by date.

No picture.

No hashtag.

Not even a barcode, for crying out loud.

I shook it with frustration. Something rattled inside.

I shook it again. It rattled again. *Yikes.*

There was *no way* I was going to open that. Who knew what might come scuttling out? Instead, I held it up to the late-afternoon sky. The light shining through the flimsy paper revealed about thirty small black things inside.

These things had small, round black bodies, out of which grew four thin black stalks. They weren't moving – they looked as if they'd dried up a long time ago. But they were spooky. Even their not moving was kind of frightening.

Here's a list of the things they looked like:

1. Small, petrified jellyfish.
2. Aliens with no faces and four legs.
3. Dried-up severed heads, with mad hair.

I stared at them again. They seemed to be waiting for me to do something. But what, exactly?

My cheeks burned. Mixed in with my fluttery sense of revulsion was a feeling of being tricked. It was like discovering that something I thought would be exciting wasn't, after all. Our Year Three class trip to the Little Sterilis dishcloth factory, for instance. (Take it from me: not the adrenaline-fuelled ride it sounds. And a very limited range of gifts in the gift shop, if you know what I mean.)

I crumpled the packet up in my hand, scooped up Mr Grittysnit's letter, stomped back inside and locked the back door firmly.

Because – and pay attention, folks, for here is an important life lesson at no extra charge – if you want to protect yourself from a mysterious dark magic against which you are totally defenceless, then bringing it into your home and locking the door, thereby *locking yourself in with it*, is *definitely* the right way to go about it.

Like I said, on the house.

CHAPTER 5

Mum had the best job in the world. She spent her days gazing at mountains of cheese, lakes of tomato sauce and a gazillion giant tubes of spicy pepperoni meat coming down from the factory ceiling like blessings from the pizza gods. Mum made pizzas at Chillz, our town's frozen-pizza factory.

Well, if you wanted to split hairs, the machines made the pizzas; Mum looked after the *machines* that made the pizzas. She kept them clean, dealt with any tech glitches and shut the factory down if they got contaminated. She wasn't a pizza chef as such, more of a machine looker-after.

Or so she kept telling me. To me, Mum made pizzas. Plus she got to wear these awesome pizza-themed overalls, covered in red and green splodges to make her look like a slice from the bestselling product in the Cheap Chillz range. (The Pepperoni and Green Pepper Spice Explosion!, only 79p. Yes, that's for an entire pizza. I *know*.) I loved those overalls; I loved even more the wedge-shaped badge pinned to their front pocket which said:

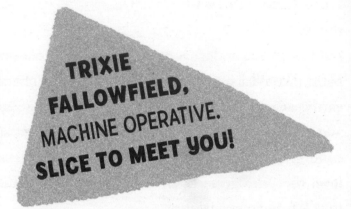

TRIXIE FALLOWFIELD, MACHINE OPERATIVE. SLICE TO MEET YOU!

As if all that wasn't amazing enough, she also got first dibs on the pizza rejects from the conveyor belts. These were the pizzas that either had too much topping or not enough, or that weren't a perfect circular shape, or were one millimetre out of the required Chillz regulation thickness of 2.1 centimetres.

Most of the rejects were pulped at the end of each day, but Mum would take as many home as she could fit into the car boot because I loved them. They were cheesy. They were spicy. They came with unidentified slices of other stuff, which could have been mushrooms, but nobody knew, and that was part of their magic.

And they were all for me. Because Mum, weirdly, never touched them.

*

Once inside, I threw the packet of Surprising Seeds on the table, got a Reject Special out of the freezer and tried to understand what had just happened out on the patio. Would I have to call the police and report an earthquake? Would Mum have felt it in the factory? Would the pizzas be affected? How could that packet have glowed, deep down in the ground? And what level of trouble was the broken patio going to land me in when Mum saw it?

It was too much. I decided to slip into a harmless little daydream just to calm down. In it, we were stepping off a plane in Portugal. Mum was beaming as she turned to look at me. And those dark bags under her eyes had gone.

I smiled back blissfully.

'Where's the pool, love?' she asked as a breeze smelling faintly of coconuts ruffled our hair. I could hear her so clearly, we could have been there. 'How was school, love?'

Er – what?

My daydream faded, replaced by the sight of a

short plump woman with bleached blonde hair. Her tortoiseshell glasses were perched on the end of her nose, and she was *rocking* her pizza-themed overalls, as usual, although she wasn't smiling quite as widely as she had been in the daydream.

'How was your day?' she asked, her hands cupping my cheeks.

I tried not to prise her icy fingers off my skin. (Her skin was always freezing – that's what you get when you work in sub-zero temperatures! Talk about a cool mum, right?)

I hesitated. *Where can I even start?* 'I think we've just had an earthquake.'

The tap gave a sad drip.

'What?'

'I was outside in the backyard, and . . . everything went super loud. I heard a chainsaw – it was a pigeon – and . . . Did your pizzas rise okay? I was worried . . .'

Mum raised an eyebrow. 'What?' she said gently.

I took a deep breath. It seemed a mad dream now; the details were already fading, and it was hard to tell the difference between what had really happened and the misshapen remains of my jittery imagination.

'The patio shook.'

'It *shook?*'

'And then the patio broke.'

'It *broke?*'

'And then I found something.'

'*Found something?*'

We stared at each other.

'You'd better show me,' she said.

I unlocked the back door and, with a trembling finger, pointed at the mess of broken concrete. 'There.'

Mum's hands flew to her face and her mouth opened, but she said nothing. She simply stood there, in her grubby white socks, gazing out at the chaos, and somehow her silence was as loud as the patio cracking.

'It w-wasn't my fault, Mum,' I stammered out.

'I believe you,' she said, turning round. 'Where were you when it happened?'

'Out by the old willow tree.'

She frowned. 'You know the rule, Sorrel. Don't go near that tree. It's not safe.'

'But I had a reason.'

I filled her in on Mr Grittysnit's important letter and the branch it had got wrapped round. But she didn't seem that interested in the letter or the competition. I mean, honestly, it was like telling a sock. But I knew, once it had sunk in, she'd be as excited as I was.

We went back into the kitchen. Mum sat at the table with a heavy sigh and took her glasses off.

After rubbing her eyes for a bit, she reached for her mobile. 'There's nothing on the local news about an earthquake.' Her bitten fingernails flew across the keys. 'Subsidence,' she announced eventually.

'Eh?'

'When the earth begins to sink it can cause tremors. Break up concrete. That sort of thing.'

She got up and went over to the kettle. 'It *must* have been the tree – it's so diseased. I bet all its nasty little roots are dying, which is why the earth around it collapsed. Promise me you won't go anywhere near it again.'

While the kettle boiled, she gazed out of the window, fiddling with the small silver hoops in her ears. 'That blasted tree,' she sighed. 'Not only do we have to look at it for the rest of our lives, but it's going to cost me an arm and a leg to—'

'*Why* have we got to look at it for the rest of our lives?' An idea popped into my head. I felt very clever to have it before Mum. 'Why can't you just cut it down?'

She poured boiling water into her mug and added milk. 'Before I was allowed to buy this house, I had to agree not to remove or harm that tree in any way. The lawyers were quite pushy about it. Made me sign my name and everything.'

She nibbled a biscuit. 'I wasn't concentrating much if I'm honest. You were a tiny baby, your dad had just swanned out and all I wanted was a home for us both.'

She gulped her tea and stared up at the clouds. 'This seemed a perfect place to bring up a baby. Wide pavements for buggies. New houses being built all the time. I would have promised to paint my ears bright purple and sing the royal anthem dressed as a banana if it meant the house would be mine. So, I signed the paperwork. More fool me,' she said, with a hollow laugh. 'But back then the tree didn't look too bad. It's definitely got worse over the years.' She gave it one last disgusted look and came to sit down, the smears of smudged mascara under her eyes making her eye-bags look even darker.

The pipes moaned. My stomach gave a queasy lurch. There it was again – that sad feeling in the house had seeped into Mum.

But she put on a bright smile and reached for my hand. 'Don't worry. Maybe it's a chance to give it all a bit of a spring-clean. We'll put down some fresh concrete and . . .' She sniffed the air with an expert nose tilt. 'Reject Special with unidentified topping?'

'Yep.'

'Fancy some of my home-made lemonade to go with that?'

'Please.'

Mum dug about in the fridge, humming, while I took my pizza out of the oven. As I cleared a space on the table, I spotted the Surprising Seeds. They were still lying where I'd left them, near the salt and pepper shakers. Maybe Mum would know what they were.

'Look,' I said, and held the packet out, but the rest of the sentence died on my lips as if I'd lost my voice. I tried again. 'Ha . . . Mmm, I foun . . .'

My lips went all rubbery and loose. Speaking proper words was impossible.

While I sat there, lips flapping about like party streamers and grunts coming out of my mouth, Mum poked her head round the fridge door. 'You okay?'

With superhuman effort, I managed to force my lips together, but this had the horrible effect of gluing them shut. 'Mmmm' was all that came out. 'Mmmm,' I said again, desperately.

'Oh, you're excited about your pizza,' she said, walking over to the sink.

I tried to call her back. 'Mmmm! Mmmm!'

'All right, darling, point made,' she said over the splutters and groans of the tap. She put a glass of lemonade in front of me. 'I'm going upstairs to get out of these overalls.'

It was no use. I looked around frantically for a pen, so I could scribble a message asking for help. But what would I write?

Oh, hi, Mum.

Only me.

I think I might be going slightly mad. How are you?

In other news, currently I can't speak because my lips have become mysteriously glued together. And I think this is all connected to what happened outside. The details are admittedly a little fuzzy, but I heard voices, thought I was being watched, and saw strange glowing things I couldn't explain.

Maybe you'd like to look into this packet

that I found – are you interested in small black motionless objects resembling jellyfish?

But back to my mouth that I can't open. I feel very weird. Can you send for a doctor, please?

Oh yeah, she'd send for a doctor all right.

Maybe I shouldn't tell her. Mum had enough on her plate. Plus, what if she confided in a friend? That was how rumours got started. *'I'm a bit worried about Sorrel'* would turn into *'Trixie's daughter is losing her marbles'* and by the time it reached Mr Grittysnit it would be *'Obedient pupil? Sorrel Fallowfield can't even make her own mouth obey her'*. And Chrissie would probably come up with another catchy nickname I'd have to grin through for a year. Mad-mouth Sorrel would probably be high on the list.

I twisted in my chair, grabbed my school bag and pushed the Surprising Seeds way down into its depths, out of sight. The moment they were hidden, my lips became unstuck.

'Testing, testing,' I said under my breath. Yep, I could definitely talk again.

'Pardon?' Mum had reappeared in the doorway in her black tracksuit bottoms and a denim shirt, a look in her eyes that meant temperatures were about to be taken.

'Nothing.'

And that was when the secret began, I suppose.

CHAPTER 6

THE NEXT MORNING, I was finishing off my toast when there was a knock on the door.

I opened it. Swallowed. Flinched. Tried not to wince.

'What was it this time?' I asked the girl with black scruffy hair standing on my doorstep.

'Hydrogen peroxide and sodium iodide.' She grinned at the memory, which seemed to make her glow with happiness. 'I threw some soap into the beaker to see how much gas was in there and BOOM!'

'Bad reaction?' I asked, glancing at the weeping raw sore where Neena's right eyebrow used to be.

'Only from Mum,' she muttered, jerking her head to indicate the smart-looking woman behind her. 'The experiment itself went perfectly.'

'*Mujhe takat dijie*,' said Neena's mum, which I know is Hindi for *Give me strength* because Mrs Gupta says it about Neena so often.

We shared a knowing look.

Neena went through a lot of eyebrows in the name of science. Basically, when she wasn't talking, dreaming or thinking about it, she was holed up in a rat-infested shed in her garden, rearranging her face with a dangerously out-of-date chemistry set from a charity shop.

*

Neena and I were born three hours apart. Our mums met in the maternity ward and bonded over a box of home-made Sohan Halwa sweets Mrs Gupta had smuggled in. As a baby, I'd never taken that much notice of Neena, being more interested in things like crying and dribbling, but that all changed at my fifth birthday party. When every other boy and girl started sobbing in my lounge just six minutes after arriving, she'd simply stared at them and went back to shaking each of my presents calmly.

One by one, the other kids were whisked away by their concerned parents – 'So sorry we can't stay,' they'd all said. 'My little angel's never done this before – must be a sudden temperature, probably got a bug or something. No, honestly, don't worry about party bags – wouldn't want to put you out . . .' Cheery Cottage had gradually emptied. Ten minutes into my party, Neena was the only guest left.

I held my breath. Our mothers hovered nervously, holding huge platters of food they'd slaved over all morning. I looked at Neena. Neena looked at me. And then she said something so wise, so profound, so comforting, that I've never forgotten it. She said: 'Cake.'

The four of us polished it all off that afternoon. Neena also sang 'Happy Birthday' to me extra loudly, helped me open every single present and refused to leave until we'd sung ten rounds of 'If You're Happy and You Know It'. From that day on we'd been best friends for life.

*

'Ready to go?' asked Mrs Gupta.

As we set off for school, Neena threw me an appraising glance. 'Something's different about you today,' she said.

'Is it my hair?' I patted it carefully. I'd taken extra time over my ponytail that morning, making sure each strand was lying flat. Every detail counted on the first day of the Grittysnit Star competition.

'No.'

'My shoes?' I pointed my feet with a flourish.

'Sorrel, they're *always* shiny.'

'Do I look taller?' I asked casually.

Neena threw me a sympathetic glance. 'Nope.' She examined me again. 'I can't put my finger on it, but there's definitely something new about you.'

'Maybe it's my face. Have I got an inner glow?'

'You what?' said Neena, frowning.

'You know, cos of the Grittysnit Star competition?'

'It sounds like a load of old methane gas to me.' She kicked a drinks can out of her way. 'A holiday means I'll be away from my lab for a whole seven days.' She stared into the distance as if she couldn't think of anything worse. 'And Mum and Dad will try to drag me out to the beach and stuff. Anyway, I'm hardly off to a great start. Not with this.' She pointed to the patch of skin where her eyebrow used to be, bright red in the September sunshine, and smirked.

Neena had a point, but I didn't want to gloat.

When we reached the underpass, she stopped suddenly. 'Hang *on*, Mum. This is important.' Her eyes raked over me. 'I know what it is! You're *crumpled*!' She stared at my grey shirt approvingly. 'What happened, Sorrel? Was the iron broken? You're nearly as scruffy as me.'

At this point, I should have just given up altogether.

Forgetting to iron my uniform in the morning was so unlike me I should have recognised it as the sign of doom it was, right there and then.

I might as well have started wearing a leather jacket and tearing around town on a motorbike, such were my chances of winning that competition.

Someone should just have tattooed ᴎOᗡ ᴙOᖷ Ǝᴚ'UOY on my forehead, which might not have looked very nice, but at least would have acted as a handy hint whenever I brushed my teeth, and saved me from an awful lot of guesswork.

But, this being real life, none of that actually happened. And even though I was totally unprepared for the malevolent dark power I'd unearthed, I still thought I was in control of my life, which was kind of sweet, while also completely wrong.

So I turned on my heel, pushing against the hordes of Grittysnit pupils swarming around us. 'I'm going home. I'll do a quick iron and run back. I'll catch up with you.'

'If you go home now you'll be late,' said Neena.

'Great,' I said bitterly as the stream of pupils pushing past us got thicker. 'It doesn't matter what I do. I'm off to a terrible start.'

'Girls,' said Mrs Gupta, 'the bell's rung. Time to go in.'

Neena gave my shoulder a sympathetic squeeze as we walked through the school gates. 'Look, don't worry about your clothes, Sorrel. You've still got the shiniest school shoes I have ever seen.'

She grabbed my hand and pulled me towards the stairs while the shrill bell clanged in our ears. I ran up behind her towards our classroom, panting a little.

Outside, the sun beat down on the empty playground. The sound of the school gates being slammed shut rang out across the tarmac. My stomach quivered as I followed Neena through the door. I touched my Head of Year badge for luck.

Showtime.

CHAPTER 7

EVERY SEPTEMBER, ON the first day of school, a very important tradition took place at Grittysnits. Before we walked into the classroom that would be ours for the next year, we'd get a special talk from our headmaster.

Oh ho, you're probably thinking. *Aha. Special talk, eh? Something to kindle a love of learning? A pep talk about wisdom and books and the wonderful things that can happen when you learn and you listen?*

Nope.

Mr Grittysnit never talked about books or knowledge or that sort of stuff. No. Mr Grittysnit liked to talk about *inventions*.

And not just any invention. He wasn't excited about toy robots, or potted plants that played music from speakers in their leaves. He preferred things that made the world tidier, cleaner, spicker and spanner. He idolised inventions that tidied up human existence and made it all a bit less *messy*.

And each classroom was named after his favourites.

This term, Mr Grittysnit had pointed at the silver plaque outside our Year Six classroom and fixed us with a solemn stare. 'There is nothing more satisfying than putting a shiny plastic sheen over things,' he'd said. 'The most boring and insignificant things in the world can be transformed with a laminator. Put mediocrity through this machine and it instantly looks better.'

Then he'd glared at us meaningfully for a while. I *thought* I heard him mutter, 'If only I could do the same to children', but I wasn't completely sure.

So, we were known as the Laminators. It wasn't that catchy. But as I followed Neena into the classroom, the name suddenly made sense. Everyone *did* look as if they'd been put through a laminator – shiny, plastic, new. It was all gleaming teeth, scrubbed faces, fresh socks. Not one grimy fingernail, stray bogey or muddy knee. Mr Grittysnit's competition had started in earnest, and it looked as if everyone in the Laminators was out to win.

'Didn't you read the letter, girls?' teased the tall, red-haired girl nearby, checking her perfect French braid in a compact mirror. 'The Grittysnit Star has to *look amazing*. Not –' she looked us up and down, smirking – 'like you've been sicked up by a cat.'

I bit my lip.

Chrissie snapped her compact shut and stared pointedly at Neena's burnt eyebrow and my crumpled shirt.

Neena shrugged. 'This will scab over soon,' she said evenly.

Chrissie looked at me with disdainful emerald eyes. 'What's your excuse, Suck-up?'

I stared at my shoes. Chrissie was the human equivalent of a funfair mirror. I always felt shorter and chubbier when she was around. How we normally interacted went like this: she'd say something mean; I'd bite my lip and pretend I was too busy thinking about something important to reply; she'd snigger, give me a pitying look and then saunter off. And repeat.

I could feel her eyes boring into me, amused. I continued to admire the view of my black lace-ups.

After a while, she laughed. 'It's your choice, I suppose,' Chrissie said casually, flicking the collar on her immaculate charcoal-grey silk shirt. 'If you can't be bothered to make an effort, be my guest. Anyway, it'll make it easier for me to win the prize.'

The scrawny blonde girl by her side nodded

adoringly, her silver braces glinting in the light. 'Easier, no contest.' I have to say this for Bella Pearlman, Chrissie's sidekick: she seemed easy to please. All she needed was a couple of words to repeat once in a while. Entertaining herself in the school holidays must have been a breeze.

I forced a smile out. *Good girls don't fight.*

After a pause, they sidled off towards their desks. As they walked away, I busied myself with my rucksack, brushing off imaginary specks of dirt.

When I looked up, Neena was giving me a funny look. 'When are you going to start standing up to her?' she asked. 'You could run circles round her if you tried.'

'It's fine,' I said quickly. 'I'd rather stay out of her way if she's in one of her moods. Anyway, as Head of Year, I can't be seen getting into arguments. That wouldn't set a good example to anybody else.'

Neena rolled her eyes as we walked towards our desks by the window. But even her Little Miss Judgy act wasn't going to get me to change. Because no good could come from standing up to Chrissie Valentini. Only last term, a nice supply teacher had gently asked her to stop losing her spelling books. Chrissie's parents had threatened to sue the school for defamation if the teacher wasn't fired, and we'd never seen the nice supply teacher again.

Mr Grittysnit did everything Mr Valentini wanted. Chrissie's father was rich, he was on the board of governors and he gave loads of money to the school every year for school trips and supplies. Plus, he owned a big property-development company that gave Mr Grittysnit a cut-price deal on school extensions, which Mr Grittysnit was very fond of doing.

So, yeah, it wasn't ever a good idea to cheese off Chrissie. Which meant pretending her jokes were hilarious. Even if they were at my expense.

*

In the Laminators, silence reigned. Everyone sat upright in their chairs, hands folded neatly in their laps, waiting for our shy teacher, Miss Mossheart, to take the register. This was unusual. Normally, she had to beg to be heard above the racket you get when you put thirty eleven-year-olds into one room.

Miss Mossheart flinched if the classroom was too loud, blushed if anybody looked at her longer than two seconds, and if she *ever* had to tell anyone off would spend the rest of the lesson panting quietly at her desk, trying to get her breath back.

You might wonder why she went to work at Grittysnits in the first place. The word in the corridor was she was Mr Grittysnit's niece. Apparently, he gave her a job because she failed her Chillz interview and couldn't find work anywhere else in town.

Her pale eyelashes peeped out through her frizzy brown hair, fluttering rapidly. She reached for her tablet and began to call out names from the register.

'Robbie Bradbury?'

'Here,' said Robbie from the desk in front of ours.

Interesting facts about Robbie:

- He's got a thing about gerbils. He managed to keep his last one, Victoria, in his locker for a whole week in the summer term before she escaped. No one knows where she got to. And this is not a book about a missing gerbil, in case you were wondering. She doesn't turn up at the end. I'm sure she's fine.
- He's totally deaf in his right ear. If he's interested in what you have to say, he turns his left ear towards you really carefully.
- Why I like him: he's funny.

'Elka Kowalski?'

A big smile spread across Elka's round face in her desk across the aisle.

'Here, Miss Mozzheart.'

Interesting facts about Elka:

- Elka's from Poland. She came to live in Little Sterilis two years ago. She and her family live two streets away from us.
- She is massively into rock music, particularly an all-female Polish band called the Sisters of Crush.
- Elka's mum works in Chillz too, but on the production line, and not in the bit where the software's kept, so our mums don't see each other much. We still give each other the odd Chillz Kidz smile now and again.
- Why I like her: I just do.

'Bertie Troughton?' said Miss Mossheart.

'Here,' whispered Bertie, making a visible effort to speak up.

Interesting facts about Bertie:

- He's a huge bookworm.
- He has quite a lot of eczema on his face, neck and hands. This seems to get itchier when Mr Grittysnit is around, and less painful when he is reading.
- In Year Four, Bertie won our school's one and only creative-writing competition. His essay was about a horrible headmaster who got eaten by a snake. The next year, Mr Grittysnit banned creative-writing competitions. But Bertie still likes doodling snakes in his exercise books. Especially when Mr Grittysnit comes into our classroom.
- Why I like him: you can't NOT like Bertie – he's sweet and kind.

CHAPTER 8

AFTER THE REGISTER, we filed into the school hall for Assembly.

The hall was buzzing. Excited whispers flew around us, thicker and faster than treacle jetpacks. Kids squirmed and craned their necks to size up their competition: other children. The air was sweet with undertones of shoe polish, iron starch and shampoo.

There was a bustling movement in the doorway. Children straightened their backs and arranged their faces into the 'nice and polite' setting.

I did the same, then nudged Neena, who glared. 'This is ridic—'

'Shh,' I hissed.

Mr Grittysnit strode on to the stage, a tall bald man in a grey suit. Everything about him was tidy and precise, from his closely clipped fingernails to the way he walked, every step exactly the same measurement as the last. Even his yellow teeth were perfectly aligned.

The only thing remotely untidy about him was the thick thatch of long black hairs which sprouted from his nostrils.

He marched to the lectern and cleared his throat. 'Children,' he said.

Along our row, Bertie started to scratch his hands.

'Good morning, Mr Grittysnit,' we said in unison.

'I have called a Special Assembly today because it is a very important day.'

I nodded solemnly.

'Now, as you are well aware, it's the first day of our competition to find the Grittysnit Star, and I want to explain the rules.'

'Pah,' muttered Neena, picking at her eyebrow and slouching in her chair.

'Rules are extremely important, as we all know. They keep us in line, give us purpose and make this school what it is.'

Next to me, Robbie nodded too, as if this was something he also strongly believed, despite the whole Victoria-the-gerbil thing, which I knew for *a fact* was against rules number 11, 17 and 101 in *The Grittysnit Rule Book*.

'Obedience Points will be allocated to every child

each time they behave in a way that befits our school's motto: *May obedience shape you. May conformity mould you. May rules polish you.* The child with the most at the end of the term will be the winner. Now, any teacher can reward you with Obedience Points.' He made a sweeping gesture to the row of teachers on the stage behind him, who looked back at us with grave faces.

Miss Mossheart gazed at her lap.

'But be warned,' the Head continued. 'If your behaviour is unsatisfactory; if you are scruffy, late, answer back, unenthusiastic about following school rules; or are dressed in anything less than our regulation uniform, you will earn a Bad Blot. The child with the most Bad Blots by the end of term will be expelled.'

There was a collective gasp from around the hall.

Bertie's fingers flew to his cheeks.

'I need not point out,' Mr Grittysnit said, his eyes sweeping the room, 'how unsatisfactory that would be. We are the only primary school in Little Sterilis, so if you are expelled, you will have to attend the extremely inferior school in Western Poorcrumble. *If they will have you.*' His dark eyes glittered and his nostril hairs quivered dramatically.

Mr Grittysnit was one of those grown-ups who could speak to a hall full of children and make each one feel as if he was talking only to them. I squirmed uncomfortably and, by the pained expressions on the faces around me, I could tell everyone else felt the same.

'But come,' he said. 'Let's not be gloomy. Follow the rules, and you have nothing to fear.'

A hand shot up a few rows ahead of us.

Mr Grittysnit stared at a small boy from Year Three – the Dirt Devils. 'What?' he snapped.

The boy stood up and gave a bow. 'My mum is scared of flying, sir, so is there any other prize we could try to win, apart from the holiday in Portugal?'

Mr Grittysnit cocked his head to one side. One of his nostril hairs seemed to peep out, as if sniffing out a potential uprising. 'There is no second prize. If you win, I suggest you put a bandage on your mother's eyes, a bag on her head, or better yet, leave her behind as punishment for her lack of cooperation. Fear of flying is simply a sign of a disobedient mind. Hers must be disciplined.'

'Er,' said the boy.

'Yet you will all be winners,' continued Mr Grittysnit, thumping the lectern with clenched fists. 'And your prize is this: becoming a better child. I have no doubt that, after eight weeks, each of you – apart from the expelled child, of course, ho ho, who will be eking out their miserable existence somewhere else – will be neater, tidier, more cooperative and more obedient than you were at the start. You will all be new and improved.'

The boy smiled uncertainly. 'Thank you, sir.' He sat back down very quickly.

'Any more questions?' asked Mr Grittysnit. 'Good. Now, before we eat into any more precious time, I have one more announcement.'

I squirmed excitedly in my seat. This term just kept getting better and better. I wished I'd brought something to take notes with.

'A school that doesn't develop is a school that doesn't succeed.' Mr Grittysnit stretched his lips back and flashed his yellow teeth at us in what we'd learned was his smile.

A little boy in Reception, new to the unpredictable ways of Mr Grittysnit's face, burst into tears.

'Which is why I'm delighted to announce that from tomorrow, work will begin on the construction of a brand-new space. A space where you will be able to reach your full potential and prepare yourself for the real world.'

I wondered what he was talking about. A sports hall? A theatre? A proper science block to keep Neena quiet? The bigger library Bertie always said we needed?

'You're all going to get a brand-new exam hall!' said Mr Grittysnit.

An uncertain silence filled the room.

Then, along our row, Bella and Chrissie began to clap.

There was a flash of mustard teeth in their direction. Mr Grittysnit waved a hand vaguely at the window, through which we could see the football-pitch-sized patch of grass that we played and had PE on. 'It will be built on that useless playing field out there.'

'But that's the last of our field,' spluttered Neena indignantly. 'There'll be nothing but concrete if he takes that away!'

'I've decided you'll be better off without it,' declared Mr Grittysnit, as if Neena had never spoken. 'Too much grass can lead to grass stains! Too many bugs *outside* leads to bugs *inside*, which leads to illness and sick days and a patchy school attendance record! A nice clean exam hall is much more beneficial to your future, your welfare – and the state of your uniform, quite frankly. Valentini Constructions –' and here those stained gnashers were turned on full beam at Chrissie, who smirked in return – 'will begin digging this week. I want you all to avoid playing out there to let the builders finish the hall as quickly as possible. And you can thank me by passing your exams with flying colours and pushing us to the top of the league tables!'

Bella Pearlman stood up and clapped frantically, like a seal who'd spotted the sardines being dangled by its trainer. 'Go, Chrissie!' she said.

Chrissie stood up and started clapping too. 'Go, Mr Grittysnit!'

He smiled at her. 'Have an Obedience Point, Chrissie.'

She smirked and shot me a triumphant look.

My heart sank. *She's in the lead already?*

Then all the other children in the hall stood up slowly and started clapping too.

'They are literally clapping an exam hall that hasn't been built yet,' grumbled Neena. 'They're clapping an infringement on our right to play.'

'I know,' I muttered, trying to look as if I knew what 'infringement' meant, 'but best be on the safe side . . .' And I got to my feet and joined in. 'Could get a Bad

Blot for not taking part. We should probably do what everyone else is . . .'

But Neena stayed stubbornly seated. 'And where are we meant to *play*, Mr Grittysnit? Next to the bins and the drains?' she shouted, but the sound of the applause drowned her out.

After we'd clapped for about ten minutes, none of us wanting to be the first child to stop, Mr Grittysnit gave a little nod, as if satisfied, and waved his hand around. This was our cue to stand up and recite the Grittysnit Pledge.

We stood and said:

'At Grittysnit, we children are
Exceptionally normal, never bizarre.
We show up for lessons five minutes early,
We eat what we're given and are never surly.
We walk and talk at a sensible pace,
With a regulation smile on our face.
Non-regulation is not okay,
That's why everything we wear is nice and grey.
Answer back? You must be mad –
To answer back is to be bad.
We love our lessons, tests and work –

Without them we would go berserk.
We won't rock the boat or speak out of line,
We won't question rules or play in class-time.
In spring, in summer, here's the truth:
We'll do our lessons under the roof.
We'll stay inside until the bell goes bong,
And that's (nearly) the end of our lovely song.
If you don't know this yet
(Have you not paid attention?),
Don't break these rules
Or you'll get detention.'

'Rousing stuff, eh?' said Mr Grittysnit, ignoring Neena's outstretched hand. 'Now run along, children, and let's start the day. You don't want to fall behind any more than you already are.'

CHAPTER 9

O NCE OUR HEADMASTER had walked off the stage, closely followed by a row of silent teachers, I jumped out of my seat, fired up and enthusiastic after Mr Grittysnit's motivational chat.

'Hey, what are you waiting for?' I asked, for Neena was still sitting in her chair, her face a thundery sky.

'Didn't you hear what Mr Grittysnit just said?' she grumbled.

'Every. Single. Word.'

'So you heard we're going to lose the playing field? If that goes, we'll have a tiny square of concrete the size of a paddling pool to play on. Does that strike you as fair? How are we all going to fit on that, for a start?'

'Oh, yeah,' I said reluctantly.

This was typical Neena, asking overly complicated questions. It was only a bit of brown earth. Perhaps an exam hall *was* a good idea. Besides, I enjoyed exams. I enjoyed drawing up revision timetables and buying new highlighters, and proving how much I knew then promptly forgetting it all once the exam was over. And was there anything wrong with that? And Mr Grittysnit had a point. Grass did lead to grass stains, and getting them out of our uniform was a real nightmare, as I knew only too well.

Neena was still looking grumpy though. 'Neena, you don't use the playing field much. You're always hunched over your science journals at lunchtime.'

'That's not the issue here,' she said. 'He doesn't care about what we actually *need* – he just cares about our stupid exam results . . .'

While she rambled on, I cast an anxious look at the clock. 9.37 a.m.

'Come on,' I said, pulling her to her feet. 'There's nothing you can do, so you might as well not stress. Besides, I've got a holiday to win.'

*

Although the others in our class were also upset about losing the playing field, things soon quietened down when Miss Mossheart put an Obedience Points chart up on our wall.

'This is so you can all track your progress,' she murmured, standing on tiptoes to stick it up next to the whiteboard. 'Uncle – I mean, Mr Grittysnit – wants it here for the rest of the term.'

'Don't forget to put my point up,' said Chrissie, touching her hair. 'The first of many, probably.'

And after that, the morning flew past, with everyone in the Laminators (bar one) trying to behave as perfectly, obediently and tidily as possible.

Just before lunchtime, with the whole morning gone and no Obedience Points under my name, my mood was pretty low. So when Mr Grittysnit dropped by and asked for volunteers to tidy up the library, my hand shot up first. I was filled with joy when he picked me. Here was my chance.

'Do you want to choose another classmate to help?' asked Miss Mossheart.

I ignored Bertie's chapped hand waggling about in the air. 'Can I have Neena?' I asked.

But Neena just scowled at me from her chair, huffing and puffing like an old train.

'Come on, this could be a perfect opportunity to earn an Obedience Point,' I said brightly.

She rolled her eyes, but got to her feet.

'Race you there,' I muttered to her as we followed Mr Grittysnit.

Neena knew I never ran anywhere in the school grounds, so this was quite a good joke. And did she appreciate it?

She did not.

*

Mr Grittysnit took us to the school library, a ramshackle collection of old bookcases in the corridor outside the kitchen.

'I want all these books covered in these grey book covers,' he said, gesturing towards a box nearby. 'They're far too non-reg as they are. And clean the grubby fingerprints off them too, while you're at it.'

'Shall we take opposite bookcases and then work towards each other?' I suggested to Neena, once Mr Grittysnit had gone. A bit of peace and quiet might sort out her funny mood, and after all the excitement of Assembly, I wanted a bit of tranquillity myself.

'Fine by me,' she said, stomping to the furthest bookcase.

Within a few moments, I'd got into the rhythm of pulling out a book, wiping it down and covering it up. It was oddly calming. I'd reached the bottom shelf of the first bookcase, Local History, when I spotted a book wedged at the back. I teased it out of its nook. It was dirty and dusty, but felt well made. With a damp cloth, I wiped the cover and a picture emerged through the grime.

It was a painting of a small white cottage in a field of colourful flowers, and the title said:

The Terrible Sad History of Little Cherrybliss.

As I stared at the cover, I had the strongest feeling I'd seen the painting of the little cottage before, but I couldn't work out where. Did Mum have it at home, mixed up with all those cookery books of hers? And where on earth was Little Cherrybliss? It didn't sound like any of the towns near us. And why was its history terrible and sad? Perhaps it was one of those forgotten villages. Perhaps it had disappeared into a sinkhole and vanished for ever.

After a moment's hesitation, I slipped the book into a grey jacket, feeling a strange pang of loss as the white cottage disappeared from view. I wrote the title on the cover, then slipped the book back on to the bookshelf.

I moved on to Hobbies. The first book I grabbed had a photograph of a boy on the cover, under the title *The Children's Gardening Book*. He seemed to be dropping something into a little pot. I peered closer. The thing flying out of his hand was small.

And black.

And small.

And . . .

Gulp.

I stared at the picture and shivered. I hadn't just forgotten to do my ironing the night before. I'd also totally *not* thrown the Surprising Seeds safely in the bin.

Which meant . . .

. . . they were still in my rucksack, back in the classroom, getting up to who-knew-what while my back was turned.

What if they were glowing?

What if they were causing the desks to topple and the ground to break?

'What's wrong?' Neena had poked her head round the bookshelf and was staring at me. 'You've got that funny shell-shocked face you get when you're panicking about something.'

I was lost in a whirl of fear. For a second, I wasn't in the library at all, but standing on a broken patio slab, watching as the world broke apart under my feet, hearing that strange voice all over again.

I've been waiting for you.

Gulping, I put my hand on the bookshelf to steady myself.

'Sorrel,' said Neena in her don't-mess-with-me voice, 'what's going on?'

She sat me down on a beanbag and looked at me sternly.

I leaned back and sighed. 'Something weird happened yesterday.'

Her face instantly brightened. 'Go on.'

I told her everything, half expecting my lips to seal together again. But they worked fine, and I didn't know whether to be relieved or disappointed. Being able to talk about the Surprising Seeds made them more real somehow, and that didn't feel like a good thing.

Neena, on the other hand, looked delirious with elation.

'Shivering silicates!' she exclaimed. 'Where's the packet?'

'In our classroom.' I shook my head with frustration. 'In my rucksack. I meant to throw it away, but I forgot.'

Her eyebrows rose so high they disappeared behind her fringe. 'You've brought *contraband* into school? You've *actually* broken a school rule?' A delighted smile played on her face.

I tried a smile and it came out twisted. 'Look, can we just forget it? Let's get back to these books.'

'Okay,' said Neena firmly. 'Once you've shown me these Surprising Seeds.'

'N-no,' I stammered. 'I can't. I don't want to.'

'Then why do you look so enthusiastic?'

'Do I?' I asked, surprised.

'Er, yeah?' she said, staring at my face so intently I felt like I was something growing in one of her Petri dishes. 'You look as excited as you do on the day of the Head of Year nominations.'

CHAPTER 10

A FEW MINUTES later, we squished between two of the most cluttered bookshelves we could find, taking turns to peep out through the shelves to make sure no one was around.

In the light of the midday sun streaming through the window, the envelope looked even older than it had the day before. I held it carefully, noticing how thin and soft the paper felt. Just how long had it been underground anyway?

'"The Surprising Seeds",' Neena read aloud in a spooky voice. '"Self-seeding be these seeds." What does that even mean?' She looked earnestly at me.

I shrugged, mystified at the sudden thrill of pride I felt. 'Who knows?'

The hot sunshine pouring in from the window bathed the packet in light and warmth. Within a few seconds it was as hot as the hottest setting on my iron.

'Ow!' I dropped it on the floor, wincing.

The packet glowed golden white round the edges, as if a thin flame was dancing inside. Then this sentence appeared: *IF YOU FOUND THIS PACKET, SOW THESE SEEDS – AND THEN YOU'LL REAP WHAT YOU TRULY NEED.*

Loads of people have since asked why I didn't throw the packet away right there and then, to which I always reply: 'Are you mad?'

I mean, what would you have done? Honestly? If something mysterious and beyond human understanding conveniently materialised in front of you one day and promised to MAKE ALL YOUR DREAMS COME TRUE?

I'll tell you what you *wouldn't* have done. You wouldn't have said: '*Hold on a minute while I run a little background check on you.*' You wouldn't have said: '*Have you got an up-to-date licence to practise the dark art of wish fulfilment?*'

You'd have rubbed your hands together and asked: '*When?*'

You know it, and I know it. So don't talk to *me* about throwing things away.

My mind spun. Could these strange old seeds be

the answer to my prayers? If they would give me what I truly needed, perhaps I needed to pay them a bit more respect. I saw myself striding into the hall, Mr Grittysnit beaming at me in a way he never did in real life, a big fat Grittysnit Star certificate in one hand, plane tickets to Portugal in the other.

BANG!

My thoughts were interrupted by the sound of something loud and heavy slamming on to the floor.

'It's only a book. It fell off that bookshelf,' Neena said, picking it up.

My heart thudded. It wasn't *only* a book. It was *The Terrible Sad History of Little Cherrybliss*. And the regulation grey jacket I'd put on carefully just minutes before had fallen off.

As if the book didn't want to be covered up.

'Sorrel?' said Neena.

'Yeah?' I gasped, with great effort.

'Your fingers are going mental.'

She was right. My fingers moved and danced in the air in front of us, as if they were playing a tune on an invisible piano. Almost as if they were speaking to me – and I knew what they wanted.

My fingers want to sow.

They wanted to sprinkle and scatter and shower and shake over. They wanted to dash and drop and dust and drip and dance and dribble. They wanted to send off and send loose and send flying. And they really, really wanted to sprinkle those seeds.

A fully formed thought bubbled up inside my brain as if somebody had planted it there. The Surprising Seeds did not want to be sealed up any longer. They wanted to get out into the world.

And I would be the one to set them free.

The shrill school bell ripped through the air and my fingers stopped twitching.

Hesitantly, I picked up the packet of Surprising Seeds, but it was cold to the touch once more. I stuffed it into my rucksack and exhaled deeply, my head throbbing.

'*Where* did you say those seeds came from?' asked Neena, her eyes shining.

I forced out a weak grin. 'Our patio.' My thoughts raced over each other desperately, like busy little worker ants late for their first shift.

I got up shakily and pulled Neena to her feet, a plan forming in my head. 'I'm coming round after school, aren't I?'

She nodded. 'What do you fancy doing?'

'I've got an idea. It's a bit . . . weird.'

Neena grinned. 'I love it already.'

CHAPTER 11

ON THE WALK back to Neena's house, we put our plan into action.

Neena went first. 'Mum, how do you go about sowing a seed?'

Mrs Gupta looked up from her mobile with a distracted glance. 'Sow a seed?' she repeated slowly, as if we'd just asked for a slice of the moon on a plate.

'Yeah. I was just, you know, idly wondering. For a friend. In theory.'

Mrs Gupta's forehead creased in thought. 'I wouldn't . . . actually know. Haven't ever done that myself.'

'Is there anywhere in town that might help? You know, a sowing seed sort of shop?' I asked lightly.

Mrs Gupta looked up at the sky, frowning. 'You could try a gardening centre. They might be able to help.'

'Is there one in Little Sterilis?' asked Neena.

'I *think* there was one here when I was a kid. It might

have closed down by now. I can't even remember where it is. Run by a bit of a character, from what I heard. Anyway, you'll have to find out yourself. I've got loads to do when we get home. A report, a couple of cold calls, a huge spreadsheet to put together . . .'

Mrs Gupta worked in the sales department of Valentini Constructions, something Neena did not like to talk about.

I persisted, knowing we'd need some options if this mythical gardening centre didn't materialise. 'What about the supermarket? Does that sell any gardening stuff?'

'They scrapped the gardening aisle a long time ago. What's all this about, girls?'

'Nothing,' we said together.

*

'Are you sure this is the right street?' I asked, an hour later.

'I think so,' said Neena, mopping her forehead and squinting at her mobile again. 'This app thinks we're standing right in front of it.'

Our plan to find the gardening centre had been going so well. Once we'd got back home, Neena had asked her mum if we could go to the corner shop to get some sweets. Mrs Gupta, staring at some numbers on her laptop, had merely nodded absently, and we'd slipped away before she'd asked us how long we would be.

'Once she gets like that, she loses track of time anyway,' Neena had said confidently. But we'd been searching for the best part of an hour and there was still no sign of it.

I was losing patience. Neena *said* she'd downloaded the right map, but it had led us to a part of Little Sterilis I'd never seen before – a rundown street with a betting shop and a large car park, and little else.

After another ten fruitless minutes of plodding up and down the same road, peering uncertainly into dusty shopfronts, I was about to suggest we go back to Neena's house to come up with a Plan B.

Then I saw it.

On the other side of the road. Nestled between the multistorey car park and a boarded-up book shop was a narrow alleyway, dark with shadows. It was so choked with weeds and overhanging creeping plants we must have missed it the first million times we'd walked past it.

'Do you think that's it?' I asked.

'Only one way to find out.'

We crossed the road. At the opening of the alleyway was a faded wooden sign hammered into a plank. Most of the words were covered in a dark green mould. I read what was left.

'STRANGEWAYS,' I read aloud. 'RUN. NOW.' I gulped. 'Perhaps this isn't such a good idea . . .'

Neena wiped the sign gently with the frayed sleeve of her Grittysnit cardigan. Gradually the rest of the words appeared through the mould. The sign now read:

STRANGEWAYS GARDEN CENTRE
FAMILY-RUN BUSINESS
NOW OPEN

She patted my shoulder triumphantly. 'This is the place.'

I peered into the murky tunnel, so tangled with stalks and leaves and hanging-down things it was hard to see anything on the other side. A trickle of icy sweat dripped down my neck. But my fingers gave a sudden twitch and burned painfully, reminding me why we were there.

'Come on then,' I said, hoping I sounded braver than I felt, and we plunged into the tunnel.

Instantly the sweat on my skin cooled. I pushed something fine and sticky away from my face and tried not to shudder.

A few moments later, we emerged in front of a crumbling red building that was smothered in a creeping twisty plant. The place was so overgrown that even the light was green. It felt like we were on a different planet.

'Hello? Anyone here?' called Neena.

Nobody answered, but I had the feeling we weren't alone. The building seemed to fill up with silence, as if it was waiting for us to say something else. Even the heart-shaped leaves that twisted round its bricks stopped rustling.

'Hello?' I tried. My voice echoed around the courtyard and came back to us. 'Oh . . . oh . . . oh . . .'

Still no one came.

Something small, black and scary flew at my face with an angry buzz.

'I think we should check the map again,' I said. 'This place is abandoned.'

But Neena shoved me.

A stooped white-haired man in faded green overalls stood in the doorway. In his wrinkled hands was a large pair of scissors smeared in something dark and red. A big black dog at his side barked loudly. The sound bounced off the crumbling bricks like gunshot, shattering the hot silence.

'What do you want?' The man's voice had the creakiness of a rusty gate opening for the first time in years.

The dog growled.

'Is this the . . . ?' The rest of my question faded in fright as he took a step towards us.

The dog bared its teeth.

'Who sent you?' said the man, a scowl flashing between his straggly white eyebrows.

Neena and I exchanged a puzzled look.

'N-no one sent us,' said Neena.

He squinted with his hand up to his eyes, as if the light in his face was blinding him. 'Oh yeah?' His gold-rimmed glasses were coated with so many layers of mud it was a wonder he could see anything at all. 'No one, my eye. You been sent by Ruthless to bully me, haven't you?'

'W-who?' I croaked.

The man carried on shouting as if he hadn't heard me, in an accent I hadn't heard anywhere else in Little Sterilis.

'Well you can go crawling back to him with the same message I tell all his lot. I'm not going to sell up. Ever. I'd rather eat a plate of greenfly than line another Valentini pocket.'

Neena and I exchanged a worried look. Was this standard behaviour for a garden centre? And why was this man talking about Valentini? That was Chrissie's surname – did he know her? I looked around the shabby courtyard, finding it hard to picture her among the broken flowerpots and rusty shovels.

The man took another step towards us.

The dog licked its lips.

'You might have swindled my ancestors but you won't swindle me.' He raised his bloody scissors and waggled them about in front of him. 'Go on, leave, before I give you a little *dead-heading* you won't forget.'

I turned to Neena. She had gone pale and her eyes were wide.

'Let's go,' she said urgently, backing away up the path. 'Thanks for your time anyway. Great to meet you.'

I was about to follow her. More than anything, I wanted to run back to the safety of Neena's house. But I remembered the words on the packet of the Surprising Seeds.

Then you'll reap what you truly need.

I needed this to work. This man could be the key to

my success and everlasting happiness. All I had to do was persuade him not to murder us.

I held out my hands and tried to look him in the eyes through the mud on his glasses. 'Look, no one's sent us. I don't know anyone called Ruthless. We're not bullies. I'm a very good girl, actually. I'm Head of Year at school.'

'Second year running,' squeaked Neena.

The man's scowl became a little less ferocious, but those blood-smeared scissors remained dangerously waggly.

'We're just after some gardening stuff.' I tried to remember what was on the cover of *The Children's Gardening Book*. 'Like some mud? And a pot? Can you help? And, oh, please could you just put those scissors down a minute – I can't concentrate while they're glinting away in the sunlight.'

The old man blinked, and took off his muddy glasses. He wiped them with a dirty hankie and put them back on his face. Although he just rearranged the grime, rather than removed it from his lenses, he seemed to see us properly for the first time. His scowl disappeared and his face softened. He glanced at his weapon and then, to my surprise, chuckled softly.

The dog wagged its tail.

'Scissors?' he chortled. 'This ain't a pair of scissors!

This, my girl, is a work of art. You're looking at a real-life, proper-job pair of pruning shears. Secateurs, if you want to be posh. Best in the business. I call her Doris. Had 'er for twenty years and she's just as sharp now as she was when I got her. Well, apart from a bit of rust, of course, but that's nothing she can't handle.' He rubbed a grass-stained finger down its blade as tenderly as if he was wiping a tear away from a baby's face.

Those smears were *rust*. I breathed a bit more easily.

'Er, yeah, she's a beauty,' I said.

The dog wagged its tail and a big pink tongue flopped out of its mouth.

The man walked a bit closer to us and a smile broke through his brown leathery wrinkles.

'Well, I must say, you don't look like typical Valentini stooges, not now I can see you a bit better,' he said.

Neena and I exchanged curious glances.

'What's a stooge?' asked Neena.

The three of us stood and gazed at each other in the hot courtyard. The old man gave us a searching glance and then, nodding to himself, lowered Doris. He took off his glasses and looked at them with a frown.

'Sorry I got you mixed up with the other lot. But these days the only folk that come here *are* the other lot, and they're a proper bad lot. I call 'em the Valentini Villains and, between you, me and the gatepost, I have to scare 'em away if I want to survive.' He lifted his chin and surveyed the neglected courtyard as firmly as if it was a battlefield. 'My motto is simple: Treat 'em like slugs; attack 'em first, before they do.'

I had literally no idea what he was talking about, but thought it was best to keep nodding.

He patted his dog with liver-spotted hands. 'Town ain't what it used to be. No more gardens. No grass. Just loads of Valentini Villains who want to keep building cheap concrete blocks with no outdoor spaces. They call 'em flats. Human hamster cages is what they *are*.'

The dog gave a soft whine. 'Don't worry, pet,' he murmured to her. Then he looked at us fiercely. 'Did you say you wanted to do some actual *gardening*?'

Now that the man's eyes weren't screwed up with homicidal urges, I could see they were a lovely light green, flecked with hazel.

'Yeah,' we said together, and I could not have dreamed that one single word would ever have made a person smile so much.

'Well then, you've come to the right place. Welcome to Strangeways.'

CHAPTER 12

'ALTHOUGH, IF YOU want to be a stickler, it's Strangeways and Son, me being the son. Mum died a decade or so ago, just after baking a cake for my seventieth birthday. Anyways, for what it's worth, I'm in charge now. In charge of a load of cracked flowerpots to be fair, but as long as there's a Strangeways in Little Sterilis, there'll be a Strangeways Garden Centre.' He clicked his heels together and beamed at us. 'Sid Strangeways at your service.'

The hand he held out was chapped and rough, with mud under every fingernail, but his handshake was warm, friendly and as firm as if he'd never waved a pair of seca-whatsits in our faces and threatened to deadhead us, whatever that meant.

'I'm Sorrel, and this is my best friend Neena,' I said.

'Pleased to meet you,' said Sid, shaking our hands vigorously. 'Oh, this old girl is Florence.'

The big black dog padded over and shoved her wet

nose into my hand. Sid looked at her proudly.

'Come to find out about gardening,' Sid murmured. 'Fancy that. Didn't think kids were into that sort of thing these days. Any idea what you want to grow?'

'We've got a packet of seeds,' I said.

'Oh yeah?' said Sid, his voice suddenly sharp. 'Where'd you find 'em, then?'

I hesitated. 'They were buried—'

'Under a load of other birthday presents,' said Neena. 'And the label's fallen off. Isn't that right, Sorrel?'

'Yeah, it's all a bit of a mystery,' I said, relieved at Neena's quick thinking. I didn't want anybody else knowing about them, especially not if there was any risk of getting into trouble.

Sid stroked Florence's head, his flecked eyes full of something I couldn't name.

'You'll be wanting some seed compost, then.' He turned towards the doorway.

Florence slowly followed him, tail wagging.

'Come an' have a look.'

*

Inside, everything was neatly laid out. Flowerpots in different sizes were stacked tidily on shelves. There were racks of seeds, bags of compost and gardening tools on shelves. In one corner scarecrows and statues stood, hopeful and silent. It all looked lovingly arranged, even though it was covered in a layer of grey dust thick as my thumb. Sid appeared not to notice. As he looked around his shop, his back straightened and his grin got wider.

Neena and I gave each other a look. It was clear no one had touched anything in the shop for a long, long time.

'Are you busy these days?' Neena asked.

'Not really,' he admitted. 'But I get by. Got my chickens an' allotment out the back. Got enough to eat. Got Florence.'

We looked around awkwardly, not knowing what to say.

'Now then, can't stand around here chatting all day – you've got seeds to sow, things to grow . . . Best get moving – a rolling stone gathers no moss.' Sid moved around his shelves, muttering to himself, leaving wellie marks on the dusty floor.

'Right, then. Well, if it's seeds you've got, you'll need this type of compost . . . and a seed tray. Have you got gardening gloves? No? Try these two on for size. And you'll need a watering can with a good-sized flower – that's what we call the thing with little holes on the top, which stops the water from gushing out all at once and soaking the earth. Seedlings prefer a gentle drink rather than a gulp – easy mistake to make but you'll be glad to avoid it and don't worry if they don't grow dreckley, cos seeds take a while to germinate. Just be patient . . .'

On he went, his stoop gone as he danced around the shop, taking things down from shelves, talking to us excitedly, giving us tips and advice and occasionally breaking off to demonstrate what we should do, his hands gesturing in the air as if he was doing the gardening himself. Florence watched him with soft brown eyes, and Neena scribbled notes next to me, occasionally butting in with questions if there was something she wasn't sure of.

All I could do was think how different Strangeways was from all the other shops I knew in Little Sterilis, with their unsmiling cashiers and massive CCTV cameras and notices that always started by saying *Polite notice* and then went on to say things that weren't very polite, like **GROUPS OF SCHOOLCHILDREN ARE NOT** WELCOME HERE or *ALL BREAKAGES* <u>*MUST*</u> *BE PAID FOR!!!*

Here, the only notices were handwritten and said things like:

SPECIAL COMPOST WORMS
ON OFFER –
GRAB A BARGAIN
BEFORE iT WRIGGLES
AWAY!

After a while, there was a heap of stuff piled up by the till. I stared at it and realised something was missing.

'Sid, do we need a spade?'

He nodded, giving me a strange look. 'You mean a trowel. You'll want to choose one yourself. Very special moment, that is, choosing your first.'

He led us to a rack in a corner, on which gardening instruments of all shapes and sizes were hanging. He gestured at them proudly. 'There,' he said. 'Meet your little helpers. See what catches your eye.'

Neena picked a silver trowel with a light wooden handle.

'Smashing choice,' said Sid approvingly. 'Carbon-steel trowel and a beautiful ash handle. Good all-rounder.'

Neena beamed.

Then it was my turn.

'Don't rush it,' urged Sid.

I looked at silver trowels, steel trowels, coppery burnished trowels that seemed to glow in the half-light of the shop, trowels with flowery handles, trowels in muted pastel colours. I didn't want any of them.

I glanced towards the ceiling, taking in the huge spiderwebs strung across the rafters. And then I saw, high above our heads and nailed to the middle beam, a small, humble-looking green trowel. Most of its paint had been rubbed off, revealing a rusty brown metal underneath.

'Can I have that one please?' I asked.

'That belonged to somebody very special.' Sid's voice was soft. 'It wasn't really on offer. But . . .'

He ran his hand through his white hair, leaving a smudge of mud on his forehead, and looked me up and down, the questions in his eyes seeming to grow louder by the second. He cocked his head and looked up at the ceiling, as if he was trying to find someone up there.

'Wants to sow some seeds, but doesn't know what's in the packet,' he murmured. 'Stood up to me when I waved Doris about . . . never done any gardening before . . . turns up here, first customers since I don't know how long . . . Spots your old trowel when even I'd forgotten it was there . . . Well, I reckon you would approve.'

When Sid looked back down, his eyes were clear and untroubled, as if the questions had been answered. He pulled a ladder out from the corner of the shop and leaned it against the wall. He looked at me as if he was sizing me up. 'Go and get your trowel, Sorrel.'

I did as he asked, carefully lifting it off the rusty nail. Once I was down on the ground again, I turned it over in my hands, liking the heaviness of it. Burned into the side of the handle was a small black *A* and the numbers *1826*.

When Sid spoke next, his voice had a crack in it. 'That belonged to my great-great-great-grandmother, Agatha Strangeways. She lived in Little Sterilis nearly two hundred years ago, when things round here were different.' He indicated the trowel in my hands. 'Back in 1826 she would have been eleven years old – your age, I reckon. She used that trowel all her life.'

I rubbed my finger along the trowel's handle instinctively. It felt smooth and worn under my skin.

'Poor Granny Aggie.' Sid smiled shakily. 'Had her heart broken by that Valentini man.'

He paused, as if he had more to say. But my mind was already racing ahead, to the pile of homework and chores waiting for me back home. I fidgeted on the spot, and he must have sensed my impatience, because he blushed and smiled apologetically.

'Oh, there I go again, waffling on, eh? I can be a right rambling rose sometimes. No point raking it all up – some stories are best left in the compost bin.'

He shuffled towards the door in his faded green overalls. For the first time that afternoon, I could see all of his eighty-ish years pressing down on his bones.

'Er, Sid?' prompted Neena.

'Yes, petal?'

'Shouldn't we pay?'

He looked at the pile of things in front of us and made a big show of doing some sums on his fingers. After a few moments, he put his hands down. 'What you got?'

'Nine pounds and twelve pence,' said Neena.

'Plus thirty-nine pence and one squished jelly bean,' I added, which is what I'd found in my rucksack.

'Well, that's a coincidence,' said Sid. 'Because all of this comes to exactly nine pounds fifty-one pence and one squished jelly bean. How about that?' He held out a battered blue tin for the money, which, I couldn't help notice, was otherwise empty.

Then, with a practised look at all the stuff by the till, he moved towards a corner of the shed. 'With all that compost to lug home, I reckon you'd be better off borrowing this.'

He brought a small wheelbarrow over to us. We heaped everything into it, including Agatha's trowel.

'We'll bring your wheelbarrow back soon,' I promised.

He gave a casual shrug. 'No bother, pet.'

And then Sid's hand shot out and circled my wrist in a surprisingly strong grip. His voice changed. 'But, Sorrel, if anything grows – will you come back and show me?'

Taken aback by the sudden fire in his eyes, all I could do was nod.

We said our goodbyes and patted Florence.

Just before we reached the overgrown alleyway, I turned back towards Sid. Shadows of half-formed questions danced through my mind. Perhaps there *were* things I should be asking. Why had he looked so startled when I'd said I had a packet of seeds? Why did he say Granny Aggie would approve of me having her trowel? And what on earth were compost worms?

Perhaps it was none of my business. I barely knew him, after all. Wouldn't I seem a bit nosy? Mr Grittysnit always said that questions belonged in exam papers, not in children.

Sid was stooped in the doorway, patting Florence and muttering softly in her ear. A strange sadness bloomed in my chest as I watched him. *A lonely captain of the flowerpots*.

I turned away. We pushed the wheelbarrow up through the weed-filled alleyway and into the road outside.

CHAPTER 13

WE PUSHED THE wheelbarrow all across town and into Neena's shed. By the time we'd unpacked it all, my Grittysnit uniform was soaked with sweat and I was covered in dust and mud.

'This gardening business is exhausting,' I panted, mopping my forehead.

When we went into the kitchen for a drink and biscuit break, I realised we could have pushed a baby elephant into Neena's shed and no one inside her house would have noticed. Mrs Gupta was right where we'd left her, playing what looked like an endless game of stare with her laptop. Meanwhile Neena's older brother was watching telly with the curtains drawn against the inconveniently bright late-afternoon sunshine.

I checked my watch. It was nearly six o'clock. The afternoon had gone. Mum would have finished work and would be driving over to pick me up. She'd be here any minute, and I'd lost my homework time. Those

Surprising Seeds were being Surprisingly Effective at ruining my schedule.

I gritted my teeth. 'Come on then, Neena, let's finish our *homework*. In the shed, I think.'

'Go steady in there, Sorrel,' said Mrs Gupta, barely looking up from her laptop. 'Some of those chemicals belong on *The Antiques Roadshow*.'

*

'First we need to prepare our seed tray,' said Neena, consulting her notebook.

'Which one's that again?' I asked, yawning.

'I think . . . Hold on a minute . . . It's this thing here.' Neena brandished a black plastic tray triumphantly. 'We need to put some compost in, sprinkle the seeds on . . . I think you'll have to do that actually – that's what the packet told you, after all . . . then water the seeds. Then we have to leave them somewhere warm . . . this shed should be good enough. They should start to grow in a couple of days.'

Start to grow? *In a couple of days?*

Neena stared vaguely at her cluttered desk, its towers of crusty beakers half filled with strange, coloured liquids, and piles of notebooks. 'I might just have to do a tiny tidy-up. Can you grab the compost?'

I gave a big, exasperated sigh in reply and ripped open the bag of compost. Nothing was going as simply as I'd hoped. Tectonic plates moved faster than this. Where was my instant gratification? No wonder Sid was going out of business.

'Er, Sorrel? Everything okay?' Neena was staring at my hands.

I was holding the Surprising Seeds so tightly my knuckles had gone white.

'Yes,' I snapped. 'Couldn't be better.' I ripped open the packet and peered in. Inside were the dried-up seeds with their creepy spindly tendrils. 'What do I do now?'

Neena consulted her notebook. 'You have to take a pinch of seeds and then lightly sprinkle them on top of the soil. Don't bury them in the earth – just let them rest on top of it.'

I stared inside the packet.

'What are you waiting for?' she asked.

'I'm just . . . I'm a bit frightened of touching them,' I admitted. The skin on my fingers was still a bit tender from when the packet had glowed in my hand earlier. What if the heat inside was even worse?

'Oh yeah,' said Neena, looking at the black seeds.

'Good point. We've already got one weeping blister between us. Why don't you just tip them out? You won't have to touch them at all that way.'

Relieved, I shook the packet of Surprising Seeds above the seed tray. I watched as they flew down on to the dark soil. 'Do you think I should say something?'

Neena raised her scabby eyebrow at me. 'Like what?'

'I just think they might need some guidance. Instructions. You know, a bit of leadership.' I bent down, put my mouth close to the soil and whispered, 'Make me good.'

It was only much later, of course, that I realised the Seeds could not care less about what *I* actually wanted.

*

Mum picked me up five minutes later.

'Good day?' she asked.

'Not bad. You?'

'It was okay,' she said, folding herself into our car. 'I had a meeting with my boss. I had this great idea for a new range of pizzas, with fresher ingredients. I even suggested a few of my own recipes – things I'd been experimenting with at home.'

'And?'

'Oh, you know, the usual response. *She'd think about*

it. Then she told me to clean a gunked-up tube that was clogged with processed cheese.' Mum stared at the pavement.

'Cool, Mum!' I said. 'If she's thinking about it, that's a good thing, isn't it?'

There was a pause. 'Must be,' she said. 'You never know. Oh, and guess what? I found someone who can fix the patio. He's coming tomorrow, with a fresh load of concrete.'

It was just what I needed to hear. Perhaps things could finally get back to normal.

CHAPTER 14

I HAD NO time for small talk on the way to school the next morning.

'Have they grown yet?' I asked Neena.

'Not yet, but Sid did say it would take a couple of days.' She grinned. 'Anyway, while we wait for them to grow, maybe we can work on *my* project today.'

'Yeah?' I wrenched my mind away from my troubles. 'What's that?'

'I want to organise a protest against the exam hall,' she said proudly.

'A *what*?'

She pulled a clipboard out of her rucksack. 'I typed up a petition last night to show Mr Grittysnit how many of us are against it. I'm going to spend my lunchtime getting signatures. If everybody signs, he'll have to think twice about going ahead. Check it out.'

She held up the clipboard with a flourish. Wincing,

I read the bold black sentences typed at the top of the paper:

Don't pave over our playing field.

Play before exams and children before concrete.

Mr Grittysnit, if being a decent headmaster was a test, you would have flunked it by now.

From:

We, the undersigned . . .

I stared at her. 'Are you insane?'

Neena's chin jutted out. 'Come on, Sorrel, this is important. Do you want to be the second person to sign?' She thrust the clipboard at me.

'Neena, if I sign your petition I might as well wave goodbye to winning that prize,' I said.

She stared at me. I remembered how fond I was of the view of my school shoes.

'Don't sign it, then.' Her voice sagged. 'I'm sure there'll be plenty of other kids who care more about their future than a one-week holiday in the sun and some stupid badge.'

'It's not just a badge,' I mumbled. 'You also get to skip the lunch queue. That's important.'

But it was more than all of that at stake. I just didn't know how to put the other stuff into words, especially not when Neena was looking at me like that, and all the other kids were jostling up next to us as we filed through the gates.

If we'd been somewhere else, I would have tried to explain to Neena that I wanted to take Mum away from all the sadness in our home, all the things that broke and moaned and howled and smelled. How sometimes it felt as if I was the only thing that stood between Mum and that miserable place.

Neena's voice rose as we crossed the yard. 'Doesn't it strike you as a tiny bit suspicious that Mr Grittysnit told us about the exam hall *right after* he announced the competition? As if he wanted to distract us all with a shiny prize before he gave us the bad news? It's like the holiday is a fat fake carrot on a stick, and we're a bunch of hungry donkeys. He's distracting us with the carrot, so he can build an exam hall we don't need over our one remaining space to play.'

'Hey, I'm not a donkey!' I protested, half laughing. 'Anyway, if he actually thought we were all donkeys, he wouldn't be running this competition, would he? Or offering the holiday, or all those amazing privileges, like having your own chair to sit in on the stage during Assembly—'

Neena snorted. 'Yeah, you enjoy sitting in your *special* chair,' she said, her eyes blazing. 'Because you won't have anything else to do, not with the new exam hall being built over the field. Sounds *brilliant*,' she said sarcastically.

Her mood got even worse when we walked round the corner and saw the bright yellow tape round the playing field. *KEEP OUT! CONSTRUCTION IN PROGRESS – DO NOT CROSS.*

'Looks like I haven't a moment to lose,' sighed Neena.

The silence between us was prickly and tense, and I was relieved when we walked into the Laminators.

*

Later, when the school bell rang for morning break, Neena tried again.

'I'm going outside to get some signatures for the petition,' she said quietly. 'If you fancy helping . . .'

I looked down at my desk, my cheeks burning. Why was she putting me in such a horrible position?

Couldn't she see what was really important?

'See you then,' she said, getting up quickly.

'Bye.'

She caught up with Bertie, Robbie and Elka, and as I heard their voices float out into the corridor, I thought about pushing my chair back and following them outside. But I stopped myself, remembering just in time the school motto: *May obedience shape you. May conformity mould you. May rules polish you.* Going outside with Neena and helping her with that petition would be breaking *all* the rules.

An odd screech outside interrupted my thoughts. I glanced out of the window to my right and saw Neena walking away from a group of kids, who were shaking their heads at her. Nearby, Chrissie and Bella were howling with laughter. Neena held her head high but I could have toasted marshmallows on the blush stealing over her cheeks. Elka, Bertie and Robbie were standing in an uncertain huddle near her, looking upset.

I took a deep breath and told myself not to move.

CHAPTER 15

By the time the school bell went, I was relieved to escape to the peace and quiet of After-school Club, where I would be spared Neena's totally unreasonable disappointment in me as a friend.

Elka pointed at the chair next to hers. 'You want to sit there, Sorrel?' she offered. 'You look tired. Are you worried about your mum? Do you want to read this new magazine I bought – it has an interview with the Sisters of Crush?'

I ignored the magazine she flapped in my face. 'What do you mean, worried about Mum?'

Elka's blue eyes went wide. 'My mum saw her crying – yesterday, just outside the factory.'

I frowned. 'It must have just been something in her eye. She loves her job.'

Elka's eyes narrowed, then she shrugged. 'My mum doesn't. Says her boss is one huge slave driver. But maybe you're right – it's a mistake,' she agreed. 'Look, check out the Sisters of Crush – they have a five-page photo spread—'

'Better not,' I said quickly. 'I think I'll just catch up on some homework.'

'Right,' sighed Elka, putting away her magazine. 'I should do that too.'

Silence filled the room. Normally those two hours flew by, as I always appreciated the chance to catch up on things, but this afternoon I couldn't concentrate on anything. Not only were my fingers *still* twitching painfully, making it hard for my handwriting to be as neat as usual, but now I had Mum to worry about.

What if she *had* been crying outside the factory? Maybe she'd been more upset with me about the broken patio than she'd let on.

I gazed up, keen for distraction. Miss Mossheart was meant to be supervising us, but she was hunched over a magazine instead, locked in a world of her own. Spotting the plate of biscuits nearby, I wandered over and, under the guise of helping myself to a piece or two of shortbread, craned my neck to see what was so interesting.

I almost dropped my snack in surprise when I saw the magazine was full of photos of flowers and plants.

Miss Mossheart looked up, saw me and shut its pages guiltily.

She blushed. 'I studied landscape design and horticulture after leaving school,' she whispered. 'It's when you design gardens,' she offered, noticing my blank look. She shrugged her delicate shoulders. 'But there's not much call for that sort of work in Little Sterilis, so I read magazines about it instead.'

I stared at her, feeling my mind grasp for something important that was just out of reach. 'You mean, you couldn't—'

Miss Mossheart sighed. 'There's nowhere green in this town,' she said. 'Haven't you ever noticed that? It's all been paved over.' She bit her lip.

I blinked, flattered she was confiding in me, but unsure what to say.

She paused, and looked up at the ceiling above her desk, as if trying to work out where Mr Grittysnit was. 'Look, don't tell anyone you saw me reading this, okay? Unc— Mr Grittysnit doesn't like me talking about nature. He's not a fan of anything you can't hoover away.'

I nodded, too distracted to say anything, and walked back to my desk, narrowly dodging one of the painful rubber bands Chrissie liked to flick at my neck.

*

Back home, there was a builder in our kitchen washing his hands at the sink.

'Well, this is the oddest job I've ever taken on, Miss Fallowfield,' he said, rubbing his hands on his dirty jeans.

'Why's that then, Vinnie?' said Mum, sitting next to me at the kitchen table as I tucked into a Reject Special next to her.

He turned round and faced us, a frown on his spotty forehead. 'Well, today I tried to take up the old cracked slabs so I could dig a new foundation into the earth, right?'

'Right,' said Mum.

'But, the thing is, before you lay down fresh patio slabs, you gotta clear the ground of weeds and plants, see. It means the foundations will be straight and level.

''Cept, every time I reckoned I'd finally cleared the ground, I only had to turn round again and a few more weeds had sprung up, right in the area I thought I'd just cleared,' said Vinnie, scratching his head. 'I spent almost all day clearing the earth, Miss Fallowfield. It seemed that the more I cleared the ground, the faster it grew. It's almost a sort of . . . mutant growth.' He paused, and glanced out at the backyard, where the ugly willow tree moved in the wind. 'So I didn't get a chance to lay the concrete down today, like I thought I would. But I'll be back tomorrow, and I'm bringing a mate to help. We'll get on top of it, don't you worry. I'm not going to let a little thing like grass and weeds stop me from doing my job.'

'Right,' said Mum. 'Thanks.'

'See you tomorrow then,' said Vinnie, walking out of the kitchen as he shot one more puzzled look over his shoulder.

I took a look at Mum's worried face, grabbed my phone and tapped out a text to Neena.

Are they growing? S x

Five minutes later, I got her reply. **Nope.**

No kiss, I noticed. She was obviously still upset about me not helping with the petition.

Oh yeah, Sorrel 'Eagle Eyes' Fallowfield – that was me.

CHAPTER 16

HALFWAY THROUGH ENGLISH the next day, as we were taking it in turns to read aloud from Mr Grittysnit's self-published book, *Be the Best by Being like the Rest – Stand Out by Fitting In*, I had the strangest sensation someone was whispering in my right ear.

'What?' I asked Neena in an irritated whisper. 'I'm trying to concentrate.'

'I didn't say anything,' she retorted.

I whipped round suspiciously, wondering if Chrissie was playing a trick on me, but she just gave me a sneer and went back to fiddling with her split ends. Then I heard it again.

Why haven't they grown yet, Sorrel? said a voice inside my head.

Once I'd got my breath back, I replied in my head. *I'm trying. I'm doing my best.*

Try harder, the voice replied. *Break the rules. Or you'll lose your chance.*

Break the rules? Break what rules? Gardening rules? School rules? Either way – *break the rules?*

It was hard to tell who was madder – me, for hearing the voice, or whoever owned the voice, for their terrible advice.

*

After lunch, we filed outside into the small square yard by the bins, where we bumped up awkwardly against hundreds of other pupils, crammed into the tiny space now the playing field was out of bounds.

'It's like human dodgems,' Neena grumbled, squishing through a bottleneck of Third Years. 'Prisoners get more outdoors space than this.'

I grabbed her hand, still shaken by the voice I'd heard. 'Look, never mind that. Have the Surprising Seeds grown yet?'

'Not yet,' sighed Neena, rolling her eyes. 'But Sid did say it would take them a couple of days to germinate.'

'*It's been a couple of days!*'

A few kids near us gave us some funny looks.

I lowered my voice. 'Look, I'm worried I'm running out of time. It's hard to explain, but—'

I was interrupted by the sound of a huge mechanical roar ripping through the air, followed by a loud scraping noise, as if our school was being shredded by something hungry.

Chrissie grinned. 'That will be the diggers,' she boasted. 'Daddy likes them to start on time.'

Neena and I stared at each other and, united by a common enemy, the tension between us melted away.

Her gaze softened. 'Come round on Saturday morning and we'll check on them together.'

'Thank you,' I said weakly. 'That would be great.'

*

Back home that evening, the look in Vinnie's blue eyes was a little more desperate. 'Well, me and Jules managed to clear all the broken slabs away,' he said finally.

'Great,' said Mum.

'And we managed to keep on top of the mutant grass and plants enough to put down the hardcore and mortar,' he added. 'In fact, we put down new slabs almost all the way up to the . . . tree.' Vinnie shuddered on the final word.

'What happened?' asked Mum.

'It was the weirdest thing. The branches kept hitting us.'

'*Hitting* you?'

'Well, every time we tried to put new slabs down round its base, they sort of . . . whacked us on the head.

At first, we thought it was kids, playing. But then we realised there were no kids playing in your yard. Then we each thought it was the other one, playing a trick. Then we got quite cross and had a bit of a barney. Then we thought it was the wind. Then we realised it wasn't the wind, cos the branches kept hitting us even when there wasn't any. Then we—'

'So, did you manage to put any slabs down by the tree, Vinnie?'

'Not today, no,' said Vinnie, touching the back of his head tenderly. He squared his shoulders up and looked Mum in the eye. 'But we'll be back tomorrow, with hard hats.'

CHAPTER 17

That Saturday morning, I was at Neena's house at 7.30 a.m.

'I'm not too early, am I?' I asked, realising that Neena was still in her Marie Curie pyjamas while her parents were standing behind her in the hall, wearing their dressing gowns and looking half asleep.

'It's all right,' Neena grinned, rubbing her eyes. 'Early birds and all that.'

'Careful out there, girls,' said Mr Gupta, wandering into the kitchen and putting the kettle on.

'Yeah, it would be nice to start the weekend without a trip to casualty,' added Mrs Gupta, yawning. 'For once.'

*

Inside the shed, my heart sank. Neena was right. There were no little green shoots, no signs of life. The Surprising Seeds just lay there, like shrivelled-up old jellyfish collapsed in a field.

I threw her a frustrated glance. 'Have you been

watering them properly, like Sid said?'

'I've done *everything* Sid told us to. I've watered them, checked on them, made sure they're covered up at night, given them heat, made sure they're not too chilly. About the only thing I haven't done is wrap them in a blanket, give them hot chocolate and sing them a lullaby. Don't blame *me*.'

'Maybe they're past it, Neena,' I muttered. 'They looked about a hundred years old, didn't they? Perhaps they would have worked if they'd been discovered earlier, but it's too late now. All that glowing probably used up whatever bit of energy they had left, and now . . . they've nothing left to give.'

Neena patted my shoulder and said, 'Never mind. At least we tried. Look, throw them away and then we can mix some random chemicals in the Bunsen burner instead? That always takes my mind off things.'

'Okay,' I said reluctantly. And, idly, I picked up the green trowel lying by the seed tray, bent over the dark brown earth and dug the Surprising Seeds up with the trowel.

wHOOOSH.

A quiver of energy danced in my bones. I felt as if I was part of something huge and strange and . . . furious.

I could *feel*, in every part of my body, that something, or someone, somewhere, was shaking with betrayal, and, underneath it all, there was a note of sadness, deep and strong and twisted with heartache. Buds of anger blossomed in my blood.

'Sorrel? You okay?'

'I – er . . .' I couldn't say any more.

A woman's voice, soft and raspy and scratchy with pain, began to sing in my head.

I closed my eyes, suddenly dizzy.

Her voice got louder.

A long time ago, I lost the fight,
But now these seeds can make it right.

I looked down at the trowel shaking in my hand, and then we both screeched.

The Surprising Seeds were no longer black and still. They were glowing. They seemed alive, each one trembling with mysterious energy.

'Holy plutonium,' breathed Neena.

The voice began again, low and insistent.

He told me this, and he told me that,
But he lied to me, and he broke our pact.

'Sorrel?' Neena said.

'Wait – I'm just – there's a v-voice –' I stammered,

before it drowned out my own words and all I could do was listen.

And now I'm dead – alas, alack –
But with these seeds I'll get him back.
Now help me right this terrible wrong
And listen carefully to the words of my song.
Ask yourself what you truly require;
Look inside for your heart's desire
Then sow yourself a seed (or two)
And what you need will come to you
And because giving is receiving (so I've found)
I've made sure there's plenty to go round
So if someone you love could do with a change,
Give them a sprinkle too, for a life rearrange.

'Sorrel, come on, throw me a bone. What's going on?'

'It's still talking,' I stammered.

'*Who?*'

I shrugged my shoulders. 'Your guess is as good as—'

The voice began again.

Now you have my trowel and you found the seeds –
You've brought them to life! You've got the key!
So, go ahead and send them flying,
And then with joy you'll surely be crying.

My thoughts felt as jumbled as a jigsaw which had been thrown up in the air and landed haphazardly.

'Hold on,' I said, noticing Neena's eager face. 'Wait. I need to think.'

Her eyes wide, she nodded.

I stared down at the trowel in my hand. The Surprising Seeds had stopped glowing, but now I was in no doubt of their power.

I sifted through the phrases I'd heard. I needed to send them flying . . . and think about the people I loved . . .

Okay. Well, I really wanted Neena to sort out her *attitude* towards school. She could do with being a bit less rebellious. This whole petition phase she was going through was a waste of her time and energy.

And me? What did *I* need the most?

Well, it was obvious, wasn't it? I needed to be myself, except more so. Better. Gooder.

So I knew *what* we needed. But *where* should I sprinkle the Seeds to make that happen?

A beam of light came in through the dusty shed window and landed on the top of Neena's head.

My brain began to spin, like a bicycle going faster and faster downhill.

'I know where to sow the Surprising Seeds!' I

gasped, nearly dropping the trowel. Now I knew why they hadn't grown in the tray.

They needed to go somewhere else. Somewhere really warm. Somewhere really Surprising.

'I need to sow them on our heads.'

Neena blinked. 'On our *heads?*'

We burst out laughing.

She caught sight of something in my face. 'You mean it,' she said, as her giggles faded. 'You want to plant them *on our heads.*'

'Well, it's just a theory,' I said. 'I guess we could see it as an . . . experiment?'

She stood up eagerly. 'What are you waiting for? Let's do this!'

I reached out and touched the Surprising Seeds with my fingers. This time, the heat inside them was soothing, rather than painful.

The shed filled with a golden light. Carefully, hardly daring to breathe, I sprinkled the Surprising Seeds right over Neena's scalp. They flew down quickly, and for a brief moment I saw them glinting, and then . . .

. . . they vanished. As if they were swallowed up whole by her head.

And for a moment, I had the feeling that something

– or *someone* – was laughing with wicked glee.

Or delight.

It was hard to tell.

Okay? *It was hard to tell*. There was a lot going on at the time.

'Your turn,' said Neena.

I imagined the smile on Mum's face as we lay on a beach. I took a pinch of the Surprising Seeds and lifted my hand over my head. Then I sprinkled them carefully on to my scalp.

CHAPTER 18

'Sorrel? Love? Fancy a cuppa? Bit of toast?' Soft fingers stroked my hair.

'What day is it?' I mumbled.

'Sunday. You've been having a right old catnap.'

'Sunday? What happened to Saturday?' I asked thickly.

Mum's smile flickered. 'Don't you remember? Goodness, you *were* tired. Well, you got back from Neena's after lunch, said you fancied a nap and went to bed. I tried waking you for dinner, and also breakfast this morning, but you were in such a deep sleep I couldn't shake you out of it. That must have been some week!' She put her hand against my forehead. 'How are you feeling? Do you think you might be coming down with something?'

'I-I don't think so,' I stammered.

'It's stuffy in here. Shall I open a window? Maybe you need some fresh air – you've been stuck inside that school all week—'

'No,' I said sharply, taking us both by surprise. 'Don't

open the curtains. I don't want any light to get in.'

Mum's green eyes narrowed. 'Why?'

'I can't explain it,' I mumbled, turning over and shoving my face back into my pillow. 'I just . . . want a bit of blackness around me.'

It was more than that. I wanted to wrap myself up in the dark. I wanted it to smother me, to carpet me. And most of all, I wanted it to cover my head. I burrowed under my pillows and gave a sigh of relief.

'I'll give you another hour,' said Mum in a puzzled voice, getting up from the bed, and I was asleep before the door shut.

*

'It's three in the afternoon. Up you get, sleepyhead,' said Mum.

With aching limbs, I got out of bed, shrugged on my old dressing gown and stumbled into the kitchen, Mum following quietly behind.

'Fancy some pancakes?' she asked.

I nodded.

Once they were done, she put a stack in front of me and looked at me warily, as if weighing up what to say next. 'Sorrel, love, I think you're taking this . . . Grittysnit Star thingummy too seriously.'

I took a hasty swallow of my pancake, wincing as a ball of unchewed batter slid into my stomach. 'What?'

Her voice was gentle. 'Look, you wouldn't be sleeping all day if you weren't stressed out. I'm worried about you.'

'*You're* worried about *me*?'

She nodded, and the small silver hoops in her ears swayed back and forth.

The tap dripped. The pipes moaned. The sound of the willow tree's branches rattling back and forth on the broken patio got louder. *Scrick. Scrick.*

I thought about telling her the truth. *It's you that doesn't seem happy, Mum. I'm doing this for you.*

But that would mean having an honest, heartfelt conversation, and we all know how easy I found those. So I said I was fine, and she pretended she believed me, and everything went back to normal.

Ha ha.

Ha.

Just my little joke.

Nothing went back to normal *ever*. Normal was waving goodbye from the boat as it sailed off into the sunset, never to be seen again, except I missed the farewells because I was too busy eating pancakes, pretending everything was fine.

CHAPTER 19

THE SOUND OF a car door banging outside had me hopping out of bed quicker than you could say 'Pizza's ready'.

I staggered round the room in a daze. What time was it? I'd only gone upstairs for a little catnap after our chat. But a gummed-up feeling in my eyes and a none-too-fresh taste in my mouth gave me the unsettling feeling I'd slept a bit longer than that.

'Mum?' I called out.

A strong wind whooshed past the house as if in answer. I ran to my window. Her rusty brown car wasn't in its usual space outside our house. Which meant she'd gone to Chillz. Which meant . . .

. . . it was Monday morning. I'd slept through all of Sunday afternoon and the evening too. I slapped a hand to my forehead. What was *wrong* with me? *Where was my motivation?*

I threw myself a glare in my bedroom mirror. And

immediately had something else to worry about.

I looked *weird*. My Cheddar-coloured hair, normally so straight and well behaved, was standing up in all sorts of weird kinks, as if I'd stuck my hand in an electric socket. My freckles seemed larger than usual, my skin was flushed and, for an instant, I could have sworn I saw the skin round my hairline . . . bulge.

I really had slept for too long – it was playing havoc with my imagination. Dry-mouthed with panic at how late it was, I ran around my room, picking up various dirty bits of school uniform off the carpet and throwing them on.

This was not exactly the brilliant start to the week I'd hoped for after sprinkling those Surprising Seeds on my head. They'd promised everything I desired. But so far, all they'd brought me was a serious case of bed hair and yet again I'd *run out of time to do my ironing*.

I staggered downstairs and shoved some bread in the toaster.

The wind howled. My confused thoughts were interrupted by a knock on the front door.

'Hello.' Neena grinned. 'Ready for another week at the coalface?'

I looked at her carefully, sizing things up. In the

Good News department, Neena's eyebrow was healing nicely and it was clear she hadn't blown up any more parts of her face over the weekend. In the Could Try Harder category, however, she wore odd socks, her school shirt was stained with ketchup and her hair, weirdly, had bits of popcorn stuck in it.

Neena caught me looking her up and down. 'I didn't get out of bed till ten minutes ago,' she admitted. 'Didn't have much time to smarten up.'

What a funny coincidence that we'd both slept in that morning.

'Come on then, girls,' yelled Mrs Gupta, shouting to be heard over the wail of the wind. 'And be careful! This gale is fierce!'

I shut the front door behind me. She was right about the wind. It was as if we were walking into pizza dough; thick and springy. With every step we took, we went back two paces.

To make matters worse, I was blinded by my hair. I hadn't had enough time to tie it back (I couldn't be bothered to, actually, I realised with shock), and the wind was whipping it about in every direction, like a super-keen hairdresser trying out their new hairdryer. Hordes of schoolchildren ran past us as our hair snapped about in the wind, and I had the unsettling idea that something small and black had flown out of my hair and on to the head of another child running past me.

Oh great. On top of everything else, I had *nits* too.

When her mum bumped into a friend on the way, Neena jerked her head to indicate we should walk behind them so we could talk in private.

'Do you feel different?' she asked, eyes blazing with curiosity. 'You know, after sowing the Surprising Seeds?'

I shook my head. 'Not especially. Although . . . I did sleep a lot over the weekend.'

'Me too!' she said into the wind. 'I didn't get up for ages. Then my brother had some friends round and they kept shouting at their stupid computer game, so I went to the cinema – it was the darkest place I could think of – and snoozed through three showings of *Really Fast Cars and People Shooting Guns Number Five*. I woke up on the floor!'

That explained the popcorn in her hair. But I still had questions. 'Why?' I asked, puzzled.

Neena shrugged. 'Because the film is rubbish?'

'No,' I persisted. 'Why were we *both* so sleepy over the weekend? And why did we want to stay in the dark?' I started to laugh. 'Do you think we've turned into vampires?'

Neena stared at me for a minute, then said, 'Leaping lipids, Sorrel, that's the first time you've made a joke this term. Are you okay?'

I lifted an eyebrow, then tried a Transylvanian accent. 'I would feel better if I could dreeenk your blood.'

'It's nice to hear you joking around,' said Neena, staring intently at the ground. 'It suits you.'

'Fangs a lot,' I said quickly.

We bent over double and I felt a strange lightness in my chest, as well as another sensation bubbling up inside me – a wild recklessness, an energy I didn't recognise and couldn't control.

It was *horrible*. I felt like one of Neena's simmering test tubes that was about to explode.

We'd reached the school gates. After Mrs Gupta tried, not very successfully, to pick dry popcorn from Neena's hair, she braced herself against the gale and walked away.

A few moments later, our smiles were wiped off our faces.

In front of us was a huge gaping hole where the

playing field had stood. The sides of it had been roughly gouged out, as if an angry giant had started eating it. At the side of the hole were two bright yellow diggers with *Valentini Constructions* emblazoned on the side.

A tiny muscle pulsed in Neena's cheek. 'They didn't waste any time, did they?'

She kicked at a clod of mud.

I tried to cheer her up. 'What did the vampire say to the doctor? I can't stop coffin!'

She said nothing.

I pulled her gently by the arm, away from the hole and the diggers, and dropped my Transylvanian accent. 'There's no point making a fuss – the exam hall will get built no matter what you do.'

She shot me a stunned look, clenched her jaw and stomped away.

As I followed her, all I could do was cross my fingers that the Surprising Seeds would start working on her soon. Her attitude really needed sorting out.

CHAPTER 20

WHEN IT CAME to calming Neena down, there was nothing more likely to settle her than a nice tricky maths puzzle, so I was pleased when Miss Mossheart handed out a paper for us to do in Period One.

I picked up the maths paper and read: *If your swimming pool is twenty-five metres long, ten metres deep and fifteen metres wide, how many cubic metres of water are you going to need to fill the pool?*

But really, for all the sense that made, it might as well have said: 'If rhubarb, pointless, hypothetical, cabbage, how many gubbins will be whatsit to fill a doodah?'

I scratched my head. I looked at the question again. The words just jumped around in front of my eyes. Who *cared?* What would be wrong with just going for a swim instead? In, like, actual real life?

I'd never swum in one before, but now I longed for a river, where the ripples bubbled softly all day long and sunlight danced on wet stones.

Even though the only running water in Little Sterilis was the storm drain we walked over to get to school, I suddenly had the strongest feeling that there *had* been a beautiful river, once. In my head I could practically see it.

They took it from me, the croaky woman's voice in my head said conversationally. *They took it from me, and they took it from you. They took it from all of us.*

Her voice made me shiver. I gulped, desperate suddenly for a drink of water. Perhaps Mum was right. Maybe I was coming down with something.

I glanced over at Neena. 'All this stuff about swimming pools and water,' she whispered, her face twisted with agony. 'It's making me desperate for a drink.'

I was about to nod, but then I was too frightened to do more than stare.

'Neena, what's wrong with your face?'

The skin high up on her forehead had puckered up like an old walnut. The wrinkles spread slowly down her face; first it was just around the edges of her forehead, but then her entire face began to wither and crease. It was as if her insides were sucking something out of her and leaving behind just a dry husk.

Then I noticed she was looking at *me* with wide, terrified eyes.

'You look terrible,' she wheezed.

Now it was my turn to touch my cheeks and forehead with shaky fingers. My skin felt dry and rough, with gouged-out grooves in it deep enough to stick a pencil in. And, what was worse, I felt as if my brain was shrivelling up too.

'I don't feel so good,' Neena moaned, flopping her head on to the desk.

Her eyes went dull, and then she closed them. A deep sigh was wrenched from the depths of her body as if it was all the breath she had left.

'Neena,' I whispered through lips that felt cracked, my tongue fat and useless inside my mouth. 'Neena! Wake up.'

Her lips opened slightly. I moved my wrinkled head nearer to her face, and thought I caught one word. 'Water.'

Yes! That blue stuff. That was what we needed. My shrivelled old pea brain rattled around in my skull with the effort of thinking. I tried to lift my arm to ask for permission to get up. It was as difficult as lifting a lorry using my finger.

I looked at Neena slumped over the desk, and knew I couldn't wait for my voice to come back or the strength to return in my arms. There was no time to waste. *We're dying of thirst.*

I forced my wobbly legs up, staggered over to the water bottle trolley and grabbed the first two I found with hands that were wrinkled and bony.

I lurched back towards my desk, yanked open the first water bottle and held it to Neena's mouth.

'Take a sip,' I urged her.

With shaking, desperate hands, I flipped open the lid of the second bottle and took a long, deep drink. The skin on my face began to swell, as if life was flooding back into me.

A few moments later, Neena lifted her head up from the desk. A pair of shocked brown eyes met mine.

'Thanks,' she panted.

'You're welcome,' I said shakily.

We exchanged a stunned look.

'All right, children, hand over your papers,' said Miss Mossheart.

As our classmates got up, Chrissie took advantage of the noise to drop by our desk.

'You might want to get yourself some moisturiser,

girls,' she said. 'Your skin's all flaky.'

'Thanks for the beauty tip,' said Neena pleasantly. 'I'll file that with all your other helpful suggestions.'

'Do you really file them?' asked Bella eagerly. 'I've always thought of doing that—'

'Oh, yeah, I file them all right. I have a special place for Chrissie's useful pointers. Really special. It's metal and round and normally sits in the corner of a room.'

Bella looked confused.

Outside, it began to rain.

CHAPTER 21

An unsmiling Mr Grittysnit stalked on to the stage in the school hall. Lined up behind him were six large grey boards. They looked like tombstones.

He cleared his throat. 'We're a week into the Grittysnit Star competition now,' he said. 'So it's time to share your progress. If you've been doing well, you will earn the admiration of your school. This is your time to shine slightly.'

The rain drummed on to the concrete outside.

Mr Grittysnit raised his voice a little louder. 'But if you don't have any Obedience Points to your name, now everyone will know. You will feel humiliated. Enjoy the experience. You can only become good by knowing the public shame of being bad.'

A few children hung their heads. The silence pressed around me. It felt suffocating, suddenly. *So many children under one roof, not making a sound.* Even the teachers on the red plastic chairs on the stage seemed to feel it too, and they shuffled uneasily in their seats.

My eardrums began to pop. I felt very unusual.

The wind blew. The rain fell. As it bounced off the yard and the rusty bike rack and the metal bins, it took on a sound that was almost human. It sounded like . . .

A war cry. Something calling me to battle. Something telling me to fight.

Whoosh. Smash. **Ping!**

Mr Grittysnit's mouth opened and shut, but no words seemed to be coming out. It was almost as if I was watching him on our broken telly at home.

A wild giggle bubbled up in my throat. Then I realised he was staring at me, as if he wanted me to do something. But what?

For a tiny second, I didn't know where I was, or why I was there. Why were we all stuck inside this huge stupid room? And what was that strange jabbing feeling in my stomach?

Neena nudged me. 'Sorrel, he's asking you to go on the stage cos you're Head of Year.' She looked worried. 'Didn't you hear him?'

Mr Grittysnit's eyes bulged impatiently.

'Coming,' I said, and stood up.

As I tried to get to the end of the row, I tripped over

Bella's foot – or had she stuck it out? – and landed face first in the aisle.

Mr Grittysnit tutted.

I scrambled to my feet, ignoring the thumping headache pounding away at my temples, and scuttled on to the stage.

'Finally,' spat Mr Grittysnit. 'Right then, tell us who is in the lead in your year.'

I opened my mouth to speak. But my mind went blank. I could not think of a single name. My thoughts felt as soggy and useless as a sandwich left out in the rain.

Mmmmmm. Rain.

'Give me the scores, Sorry,' said the cross-looking man next to me. 'Tell me which child is winning, and which child is losing.'

Frantically, I looked to Neena for help.

With wild gestures, she pointed at a red-haired girl on the same row. I stared at the girl. *I know her. I know her name. This man standing here seems to want a name. I will say it, and then I can leave and drink some water. Because I am thirsty again, which is a tiny bit worrying.*

'Kissy,' I said.

'What?' thundered the man.

'Kissy,' I said desperately. 'Kissy. One Kissy.'

'Control yourself,' said the man, face white, eyes bulging. 'Just a name will do.'

'Kissy,' I said.

The hall burst into nervous peals of laughter, all apart from Neena, who was staring at me with concern, and the girl called Kissy, who had crossed her arms tightly and looked angry. What had I done wrong? And how did she get her hair to look so nice in that lovely way and – Oh dear.

I really was terribly parched.

A little voice from the front row said, 'What's happened to her face?'

Oh no.

It was happening again. The drying and cracking and shrivelling. I spread my fingers like a secret to hide what I'd become. The dry, dead feeling spread throughout my body, from my head downwards, and I felt it inch towards my heart. My breath was ragged.

Any minute now, I'll fall down on the stage and never get up again.

Through the gaps in my fingers, I saw a girl with white bits in her hair shout, 'Sorrel! Outside!' Then she stumbled towards the fire exit.

I staggered off the stage towards the double doors. We pushed and heaved, retching with the effort of it. Finally, they opened and we lurched outside. The rain fell over me in a cool embrace. I opened my mouth wide and I drank it in, while my entire body sang with relief. The drops seemed to kiss my face and head as fondly as a mother who hadn't seen her child for a while.

'Feel a bit better?' asked Neena. She was soaked from head to toe and grinning.

I held my arms up to the sky and did a little dance, my scalp tingling with joy.

'Is it just me, or does the rain seem a bit different?' asked Neena.

'Different?'

'Yeah. Taste it.'

I opened my mouth and drank a big mouthful. She was right. For a start, it felt softer, velvety. And it *tasted nice*. This rain was sweet, rich, with strange traces of chalk and stones, secret and faraway places.

'It's as if I can taste every single trace mineral that has ever made up this rain. All the different rivers and lakes – all the different compounds . . . magnesium . . . chalky calcium . . .' Neena was saying in between mouthfuls of the stuff.

I took another gulp. '*I* can taste worms, and pebbles,' I said delightedly.

And then the rain stopped.

'. . . have been calling you inside for five minutes,' shouted Mr Grittysnit. 'Absolutely disgraceful behaviour. How dare you ignore me? Get back inside at once and come to my office immediately.'

'Uh-oh,' said Neena, licking rainwater off her lips, while fear stamped big black boots over my short-lived happiness.

CHAPTER 22

A LITTLE POOL of water had formed by my feet on Mr Grittysnit's office carpet. He stared at it with distaste for a moment then dabbed at his forehead with a hankie.

'In all my years at this school,' he said, his voice low, 'I've never seen such an appalling carry-on.'

I hung my head, biting my lip to stop from crying. A drop of water rolled down my nose and landed in the puddle. I hoped he hadn't noticed.

'As for you,' he said in a heavy voice, turning to me. 'Head of your year. Meant to be a role model. Have you lost your mind? Behaving bizarrely on the stage, speaking gibberish and then running outside into the pouring rain and –' his mouth bulged with words that seemed to disgust him, as if he was a Hoover that had sucked up something revolting – 'dancing and cavorting in the rain. Laughing as you ruined your school uniform. Behaving out of turn. Who gave you permission to go outside and do what you wanted? Who? *Who?*'

For a split second, my brain fizzed and popped with the sound of a million tiny things shouting out the answer. *We did, we did.*

I closed my eyes and willed the sound of the voices – whatever they were – to go away.

'Nobody, sir,' I whispered.

'You're right there, Sorry. Nobody.'

But the million tiny voices wouldn't shut up inside my head.

You're the nobody, with nothing inside.

When we're fully grown, you'd better hide.

'Girls, what is our school motto?' asked our headmaster.

'*May obedience shape you. May conformity mould you. May rules polish you,*' I whispered, while Neena said nothing.

Fortunately, Mr Grittysnit seemed not to notice Neena's silence, as he gazed at the ceiling with a proud smile. 'Obedience. Conformity. Rules. Beautiful, upstanding things. They exist to knock you into shape for the world out there.' He flapped his arm in the direction of the big muddy hole outside his office. 'But you two are in *no shape at all*. You're shapeless blobs.

Conformity has not moulded you. Obedience has not shaped you. And unless you knuckle down to these superior forces, you will *never fit in. Here, or anywhere.*'

I stared at my little carpet puddle. I wanted to dive into it and drown. I felt like a pizza reject from Chillz, kicked off the conveyor belt, made all wrong.

He moved back to his desk and sat down heavily.

'You are both suspended for the rest of the day. Go home. Dry off. Come back tomorrow. *Be normal.*'

We turned to go, feet squelching on his carpet. Even though I was still shaky from being told off, relief flooded my veins. Mr Grittysnit was still talking, but all I could think was how lucky I was – sending us home early wasn't too bad a punishment, not really, not when he could have given us a—

'Bad Blot each,' he said quietly. 'And, Fallowfield, you are relieved of your Head of Year duties. It is clear you're not up to the job. I've lined up a better replacement.'

My heart dropped, heavy as an anchor. What had he meant, *relieved of my duties*? I didn't feel relieved. I felt terrible. And what was the last thing he'd said? Something about being replaced?

'But . . . Who?'

He stared at the novelty pencil sharpener on his desk. It was in the shape of a yellow digger.

No!

'Shut the door on your way out,' said Mr Grittysnit.

*

We hadn't even been allowed back into our classroom to collect our school bags.

'I don't want your sobs distracting your classmates,' Mr Grittysnit had told us. 'Go straight to the school office and wait for your respective parents to pick you up.'

I was rain-soaked and miserable. I wasn't in the mood to chat. But Neena was fidgeting about in her chair and mumbling things like 'Of course!' and 'So obvious!' to herself.

Finally, she turned to me, her face glowing. 'Are you thinking what I'm thinking?'

'I doubt it,' I sniffed.

'Our symptoms hold the answer!' She held out one hand and began to count things off on her fingers, eyes blazing. 'Yesterday, we couldn't stay awake. We wanted to be somewhere dark. Today, we were thirsty and only felt better when we were drinking water. Why do you think we're feeling so unusual, Sorrel?'

'Food poisoning?'

'No!' she said, hopping to her feet and dancing in front of me. 'It's the Surprising Seeds! They're working!'

A wave of hot anger rushed through my body, sweeping aside every other emotion. I felt tricked. It couldn't be the Surprising Seeds. They were meant to give me what I *needed*, not turn my face into a shrivelled walnut and make me prance in the rain.

'It's not the Seeds,' I said firmly. 'We're just coming down with something, that's all. We need rest. We'll be back to normal tomorrow.'

The sound of the diggers as they bit away at the earth roared in through the window.

Neena listened solemnly for a while then turned back to me. 'And that will be a good thing, will it?'

CHAPTER 23

WHEN SHE CAME to pick me up ten minutes later, Mum looked pale and tired.

'I came as soon as I could,' she spluttered to Mrs Pinch. 'It was hard work, getting out of my shift – my boss was not impressed, I can tell you. Was it really necessary to pull Sorrel out of school just because of a bit of excitement about the rain?'

'Oh yes.' Mrs Pinch nodded, her beehive moving up and down slowly, lips pursed as if she was trying not to enjoy herself. 'It was very disruptive behaviour. It's simply not tolerated here. Not when there are other children to think of. Where would we be, if they all started dancing outside whenever they wanted?'

'Come on,' Mum said heavily. 'Let's go home.'

*

'Drink that,' she said back at Cheery Cottage, putting a mug of tea in front of me. 'And tell me what happened.'

We were in the lounge, listening to the soft raindrops

beat against the window. The tea burned my throat but did calm me down.

'I can't really explain it. I was just sitting in Assembly when I needed a drink and . . . I went outside into the rain. And I sort of danced in it.'

'Wow,' she said softly. 'I haven't done that since I was a kid. Tell me what it felt like.'

This was not going well. I just wanted her to tell me off like a good grown-up, so I could get on with my life. I didn't want her to stare into space sadly and make things more confusing.

'Well, it felt good, at the time. It felt *brilliant*.' A smile spread across my face as I remembered. 'It tasted great too, and it sort of stopped me from dying.'

Mum frowned.

'Of *boredom*,' I added quickly. 'But that's not the point, is it, Mum? I've seriously messed up my chances of winning the competition.'

Her mouth sagged like one of our sofa cushions, which made me feel even worse. *This holiday means so much to her, I can tell. And now I've let her down.* I'd forced her to leave a job she loved early to come and pick me up. Plus I'd lost my Head of Year badge *and* earned a Bad Blot – in just one day! Why wasn't she shouting at me?

'Sorrel,' Mum said quietly. 'Listen, love, I don't really care about—'

Her mobile rang.

She stared at the screen and frowned.

'Oh great,' she said. 'It's my boss. Hold on a sec.'

She grabbed the phone and walked over to the corner of the lounge, dropping her voice in that way she always did when Mrs Grindstone rang, as if they were playing Chinese whispers.

I gazed out of the window as the rain splashed on to the pavement outside.

'Yes, I will make up the extra hours . . . I can't help being a single parent . . . emergency at school . . . If you insist . . . on reduced pay? Of course, whatever you think is best. Goodbye.'

Mum clicked a button on her phone and stared at her screen, sighing. She was so quiet, my brain began to wander.

I went into the kitchen and ate some crisps and tried to work out a strategy to make things all right again.

I didn't have *time* for this emotionally confusing post-mortem on why I'd been sent home early. Instead, I needed to get back into Mr Grittysnit's good books. My chat with Mum would have to wait. She seemed a bit preoccupied anyway, slumped on the sofa like that.

'I'm just going upstairs for a while,' I said.

'Okay, love,' she said, smiling brightly, but I wasn't fooled.

Her voice was as stripped down and colourless as a pizza base without any toppings. Even though she was doing a good job of holding it in, she was clearly furious about my behaviour at school.

Look, I never said I was Sherlock Holmes, okay?

CHAPTER 24

A FEW HOURS later, my room looked like I'd been having a snowball fight with myself.

I'd decided to make a start on some homework. Mr Grittysnit had set every child at the school a personal essay to write. Subject: *Why I should win the Grittysnit Star competition*. Normally, I could have written this in my sleep. But things weren't going so well.

'Aaargh!' I shouted in frustration, ripping out my fiftieth attempt to compose something meaningful. I threw it across the room to join the other screwed-up balls of white paper.

Every time I pressed my pen down on the paper, the sentence I *wanted* to come out would be replaced by rude and cheeky compositions seemingly from nowhere.

In my handwriting.

In despair, I picked up the nearest discarded sheet of paper. I'd meant to write *Please consider me for the prize* because I've always been good. But instead, I'd scrawled: *Please turn your silly old face this way a bit so I can pelt it with food.*

Gulping, I read my latest attempt. I'd tried to write *I think you'll find that my school attendance record is second to none.* But my formerly trusty biro had refused to do my bidding, and instead, the following words had come out of its nib, in a wild scribble: *I think you'll find that bullies with hairy nostrils deserve a stink bomb.*

Tears of frustration rolled down my face. I couldn't hand that in. I was doomed.

Those Surprising Seeds had promised me they'd bring me what I required. When were they going to just *get on with it* and stop wasting my time? Speaking of which . . . I glanced at the clock. It was five in the afternoon, but the house was so quiet it could have been midnight.

I opened my bedroom door cautiously. All I could hear was a gentle snoring coming from below.

I padded down the stairs. Mum was slumped at the kitchen table, asleep, her blonde spiky hair resting on a notebook. I peered over her shoulder. One nail-bitten finger lay just below a sentence she'd written: *Muffins to cure melancholy.*

The sour-lemony taste of guilt flooded my mouth. If I hadn't been suspended, she wouldn't be looking for happiness in muffins. Between her eyebrows were deep frown lines, which even sleep hadn't erased. I reached out to stroke them away.

But as my fingertips brushed her shoulder, the kitchen took on a dreamlike quality. The light shimmered. Outside, the willow branches scraped feverishly against the concrete. SCRICK. SCRICK.

Something's about to start talking to me again, I thought, shivering.

Right on cue, a chanting began in my head.

All hail Sorrel Sprinkleseed; she comes to us once more.

All hail Sorrel Sprinkleseed; she's going to make us soar.

Somehow I knew, without anyone telling me, that this was the sound of the Surprising Seeds.

A wild cackle began in my throat, and my fingers twitched in the air.

Mum slept on.

Change her fate – it will be great, of that we're almost sure.

But the packet was empty – wasn't it? I'd used up all the Seeds on Neena and me. *Still, no harm in double-checking.*

I ran upstairs and flung myself at the mattress and pulled the packet out from its hiding place.

It was full. Completely full.

I stared at it for a while, wondering how on earth an empty packet could refill itself, until the burning sensation in my fingertips made thinking impossible.

I ran back downstairs and emptied the entire packet over Mum's black roots, and the tingle in my fingers vanished. Her short blonde hair glowed for a second, as if lit by an invisible match, and then the seeds disappeared, swallowed up by her scalp.

Mum slept on.

CHAPTER 25

ALLOW ME THIS interruption to ask you a few tiny questions about your health. Nothing to worry about! Just standard procedure!

So, how do you *feel*?

Have you experienced any of the following symptoms over the last few days? Like, I don't know, wanting to sleep in a darkened room, or finding it hard to quench your thirst?

If so, here's what to do.

Erm . . .

Er . . .

Give me a sec . . .

Sorry. I have nothing. No advice. No tips. You can't prevent it.

There's literally nothing you can do apart from keep reading. At least then you'll know what to expect.

*

Anyway, back at school the next morning, things went from bad to worse.

It started with my neck.

We'd opened up our books for a bit of geography. As I tried to read a paragraph about something or other, my neck went rogue. Instead of falling forward, it moved in the opposite direction until my face was tilted up. I found myself staring up at the skylight in the middle of our classroom's ceiling.

I quietly tried to right myself and pushed my head back towards the book.

I'm in charge here.

My neck moved slowly backwards again in a way which plainly said, '*Don't make me laugh.*'

And there I was, looking at the murky mildew of the skylight once more.

'Something interesting up there, Sorrel?' murmured Miss Mossheart.

'Got cramp,' I whispered.

Neena then did me a favour by distracting Miss Mossheart and everyone else from my neck with some outlandish behaviour of her own. She pushed her chair back and stood, straight-backed and stiff-legged, in the aisle. She was also staring up at the skylight, with a funny faraway look in her eyes as if she was trying to remember the boiling point of liquid nitrogen.

'Girls,' said Miss Mossheart quietly. 'Come on now. Enough of that. Sorrel, look at your book. Neena, get back in your chair.'

I clasped both hands behind my head and pushed hard. After a few difficult seconds, my neck moved slowly back towards the book.

Aha! I thought triumphantly.

But to my horror, I felt it tip backwards again. I put my hands behind my head and pushed it back towards the book once again. Then I kept them there. Just in case the neck got any more funny ideas.

I tried a casual, carefree smile, one that hopefully said, *'This is all totally normal – nothing to see here.'*

Chrissie and Bella sniggered.

Shooting pains darted up and down my arms. My smile grew strained.

I glanced sideways at Neena. Still standing, her body swayed lazily.

'Sit down, Neena,' said Miss Mossheart, sounding close to tears.

I couldn't blame her – I fancied shedding a few myself. My best friend was going crazy and my neck wasn't that far behind.

'I can't sit down,' said Neena, her voice as soft as melted butter. 'I want to stretch – and feel the light.'

'Sit down, Neena,' I hissed. 'Control yourself.'

Miss Mossheart and I both sighed with relief as Neena bent her legs.

But, shrugging as if to say this was all beyond her control, she jumped on top of our desk and stood, basking in the faint light pouring in from the skylight. She closed her eyes and gave a deep sigh.

'I think I'll stay here, if that's all right with you,' Neena said dreamily. 'Lovely and warm. Nice bit of photosynthesis.'

My classmates had dropped all pretence of working and were staring at Neena with mouths as wide as frogs.

My neck started to twitch. But I didn't want to go towards the light; I didn't want anything to do with that mouldy glass and its dead leaves. I wanted to just sit right where I was and be perfectly normal and . . . oh.

That was strange.

Didn't that beam from that skylight look nice?

In fact, the more I peered at it, the richer and more golden it got. It looked as warm and rich as a bath of melted chocolate. What had I been thinking, writing it off as a mere skylight? It was clearly a portal to bliss.

The top of my head went all prickly, as if tiny little goosebumps were breaking out all over my scalp. It was as if it was *itching for the light.*

'Neena, get down,' said Miss Mossheart miserably.

Neena simply turned her head to the right, then the left, like a sunbather changing position.

The goosebumps on my head felt painfully tender. When you get cold, you put a jumper on. When you have goosebumps on your head, what are you meant to do?

Find the sunshine, find the sunshine, said a million tiny voices inside my head.

The silence in the classroom grew taut and tense, as everyone looked from Neena to me to Miss Mossheart, waiting to see what would happen next.

I gripped my desk with both my hands, determined to stay in my chair. Sweat began to bead on my forehead.

I couldn't fight it any longer. After a few more

seconds of agony, I pushed my chair back and vaulted on top of the desk. It wobbled slightly, but managed to bear my weight.

Somebody laughed. But I didn't care.

I bent my head. The light washed over me, gentle and soft, and every single hair follicle on my head seemed to gobble it up. A few seconds later, a deep, wonderful heat began to pulse around my brain and radiate out towards my face. I shivered with joy and every other thought disappeared.

CHAPTER 26

IT TOOK FIVE minutes, and a lot of begging from Miss Mossheart, for us to be coaxed off our desks and back into our seats.

'You're being too soft on them, Miss Mossheart,' said Chrissie, stroking her Head of Year badge and looking at me with a smirk. 'Send them home. The Grittysnit Pledge clearly states that we won't "play in class-time".'

Miss Mossheart gulped and pretended she hadn't heard her.

'No backbone, that's her trouble,' Chrissie grumbled.

An ear-splitting shriek tore through the air, and everybody turned to look at me.

'What *now*, Suck-up?' tutted Chrissie, her sharp face mottled with frustration. 'Haven't you had enough attention today?'

'Thought I was stung by a bee.' I rubbed my prickling scalp as subtly as I could.

'Are you okay?' whispered Neena.

'Dunno,' I spluttered, feeling confused and embarrassed.

Didn't bees only sting if you sat on them, or something? And why hadn't I heard anything buzzing before the sting?

As I rubbed my scalp again, it soon became worryingly clear that those little goosebumps I'd felt earlier were bigger and they were all over my head in a rash.

'AAARGH!' shouted Neena, rubbing her head vigorously. 'I've been bitten too!'

'Oh, *please*,' said Miss Mossheart in the panicky, despairing way of a woman on the edge.

While Neena hopped about, rubbing her head, I was bitten again. I held my hands over my head and ducked down, but despite throwing panicky glances around the room, I couldn't see the bees.

Perhaps they were invisible.

Invisible bees?

Also, why were they only singling out me and Neena? Everybody else seemed unharmed.

Through the pain, I heard a small voice of doubt in my head.

Most insect bites, as far as I could remember, felt like something trying to bite their way *in*.

But this felt as if something was trying to push its way *out*.

And not just one thing. Loads of them.

As if a million little knitting needles were trying to burst through the skin on my scalp. I wanted to tear my skull open to get rid of the pain. I raked my fingers through my hair, flinching at the size of the swellings. They had got even larger.

Chrissie made a gagging noise. 'Bees, my foot! You probably have fleas.' She raised her voice. 'Miss Mossheart, Neena and Sorrel are health and safety risks. They're *riddled* with parasites. Shouldn't you send them home?'

I hung my head with shame.

BRIIING!

The school bell ripped through the air, breaking the suspense.

Miss Mossheart's face collapsed with relief. 'Class dismissed,' she moaned. 'I'm just going to have a little cry – I mean, a cup of tea somewhere quiet.'

Once she'd run out of the door, the whole classroom erupted.

'Are you okay?' asked Elka, looking as if she wanted to come closer but throwing concerned glances around the room.

'Can I get you anything?' murmured Robbie.

'I can lend you some of my eczema cream.' Bertie blushed. 'It might help with the stings.'

Only Chrissie gave us a scowl, which made her sharp face uglier than usual. 'Ridiculous attention-seeking tactics.'

'Tic Tacs,' said Bella sternly.

'Sorrel,' hissed Neena, grabbing me by the hand. 'Come to the toilets with me. We need to *talk*. Now.'

*

Once we were sure we were alone, we turned to each other in front of the sinks.

'*Now* do you believe me?' asked Neena.

'About what?' I said, puzzled.

'What did I try to tell you yesterday, just before we got sent home?'

I stared at her.

'Come on, *think*.'

Finally, I understood. 'It's not the Surprising Seeds – it can't be!' Quickly, I explained. 'Before I sprinkled them on our heads, I heard a woman . . . singing at me. And this *voice* said the Surprising Seeds would give me what I wanted – or needed. Anyway, it's more or less the same thing. So it can't be the Seeds!'

But my brilliant argument seemed to be wasted on Neena, who was simply staring at my forehead and gasping.

My fingers flew up and met something soft, with little delicate tendrils. Confused, I stared at myself in the mirror.

I no longer had any skin on my forehead. Instead, I had moss. Dark green and soft. My forehead was covered in it. Right up to my eyebrows. There was basically a small lawn on my face.

So that was a new look.

Then things got worse.

A small green stem began to poke out of my scalp.

It was joined by another.

And another.

And then a hundred more.

They shot up quickly and unfurled at the top, like little flagpoles being unveiled.

Those painful swellings on my scalp had been tiny green stems, just waiting to burst.

I gasped as the stems grew longer and longer,

stretching up towards the bathroom ceiling. When they were roughly the height of my finger, they stopped growing. Tiny blue flowers extended slowly from the tops of the stems. And red flowers. They opened proudly and then began to wave about in the air, as if saying hello to each other.

'Make them stop!' I said in a begging voice, my hands flying all over my head as I tried to squish the flowers back down again.

But Neena just stood there, gasping and looking as if she wanted to clap.

Within a few seconds, my entire scalp was covered. I looked like a flowery pincushion.

I grabbed a handful of flowers and tried to rip them out, but although I tugged and pulled till my eyes watered, they remained firmly rooted in my skin.

As I stared in dismay at my reflection, the last remaining patches of my hair went from Cheddar yellow to . . .

. . . green.

'You've got *grass for hair.*' Neena sounded delighted.

Still the girl in the mirror continued to grow ever more freakish. My eyebrows turned into daisy stalks. My eyelids turned into tiny red leaves and little bright purple flowers burst open on my nose.

I moaned with shock as my fingers crept slowly up to my face, to feel and to prod, but at the very last minute, I pulled my hands back. I couldn't bear to touch any of it.

'Holy hydrocarbons,' said Neena, her mouth hanging open. 'You look awe—'

And then she stopped and clutched her scalp, and her eyes grew wide.

'My turn,' she said, with what looked like a smile flickering about her face.

*

Now it was my turn to stare. Over the last few minutes, Neena's scruffy black hair had receded, and in its place an entire vegetable plot had popped up, with rows of red tomatoes and tiny creamy potatoes. Neena reached up, plucked a tomato from her head and popped it into her mouth.

As she stared at herself, munching, I moaned and clutched the sink. 'We are going to be in so much trouble.'

'Have a tomato,' said Neena. 'They're very good.'

'How can you be so calm?' I yelled. 'Our heads have mutated! Aren't you upset? Aren't you confused? Don't you want to know why this is happening to us?'

Neena gave me a firm but kind look. 'Oh, Sorrel, I've been trying to tell you for ages,' she said. 'It's the Seeds, dummy. They've finally grown.'

CHAPTER 27

'THINK ABOUT IT. Neither of us knows much about gardening, but we do know that plants need water and sunlight to grow, right?'

I gave a miserable nod and the flowers on top of my head bobbed up and down.

Neena grinned at them and then, noticing the look on my face, stopped. 'Sorry. Anyway, after you sprinkled the Seeds, we really wanted to be in darkness, didn't we? That was probably the Seeds wanting to – what did Sid call it? Germinate? And then, once we'd slept and found a bit of darkness, do you remember how thirsty we were?'

I moaned at the memory of us dancing in the rain.

'So that would have been the Seeds needing water to grow. And then, this morning, how we felt about that funny old skylight – what do you think that was?' Neena's voice was patient but determined.

'The Seeds wanting sunshine?' I suggested reluctantly.

'Full marks to you! This is all the Seeds, Sorrel. It's not a bug!' Neena clutched my arms, her eyes bright. 'It's our experiment reaching its perfect conclusion!'

I had to admit Neena was right. In which case . . .

That voice. The voice had lied to me.

I frowned, remembering what I'd heard in Neena's shed.

Go ahead and send them flying, it had said.

And then with joy you'll surely be crying.

Well, I certainly felt like crying, but it wasn't with joy. What else had it said?

Sow yourself a seed (or two),

And what you need will come to you.

Well, that was another whopper for a start. I'd been tricked. But why?

'We need to get home before anyone spots us,' I gibbered, frantic with fear at being caught. 'We need to find a way of getting rid of it all.'

The caterpillar crawling around Neena's forehead turned and gave me an angry glare. I tried not to look at it.

'And we have to get out of here *now*, before anyone sees us—'

The door slammed open, and Chrissie's perfect face peered round.

'Too late for that,' she said, her voice dwindling in shock as she saw our heads. She swallowed, regained her composure and rolled her eyes. 'I've been sent to find you as you're running late for Spanish. And *you* can tell Miss Mossheart why you've decided to have a little game of Dress Up in the toilets.'

*

Chrissie led us down the corridor, opened the classroom door and jerked her head at us.

I slunk in, trying to make myself as small as possible, but Neena simply strode in, grinning away.

Elka stared at us and gasped.

Bertie opened his mouth to say something, then went bright red and shut his mouth again.

And then everybody began to howl with laughter. Which, of course, happened at exactly the moment Mr Grittysnit walked past the Laminators, because those Surprising Seeds knew a thing or two about timing.

By which I mean they knew how to time things *really badly*.

CHAPTER 28

HE GLARED AT Miss Mossheart in fury. 'Milly, control your class.'

Then he saw us.

He ogled. He stared. His eyeballs swelled so much, it was as if he'd stuck bloodshot party balloons in his eye sockets for a dare.

'Take off your hats,' he said ominously.

'They're not hats,' said Neena.

'Take them off at once,' he repeated.

'We're not wearing hats,' Neena said, her voice low, her eyes steady.

'If you don't take those hats off immediately, I'm going to come over there and remove them myself,' he snapped in a voice that crackled with fury.

Neena yawned.

He stalked over and put his hands round Neena's allotment head. He tugged and he pulled and he groaned and his eyes bulged with the effort but all he succeeded in doing was getting mud underneath his fingernails.

'What have you put it on with – glue?' he asked.

'Nope,' said Neena.

'I'll get this hat off if it's the last thing I do,' he muttered, face red and sweaty, and he wrapped his hands round one of the green shoots sticking out of Neena's head.

His mouth and eyes screwed up in concentration as he pulled. Eventually, there was a soft sound of something giving way, and the shoot began to loosen.

Neena winced, but stayed quiet.

'Aha,' grunted Mr Grittysnit in satisfaction. 'Getting somewhere now.'

'Certainly sounds promising,' said Neena.

'If I have to pull it off thread by thread, that's what I'll do,' he said, giving one final tug.

There was a horrible sound of something ripping and I closed my eyes.

A few seconds later, I opened them again, to find that Mr Grittysnit was holding a very small but perfectly formed carrot, dangling on the end of a green shoot covered in mud. He glanced at it with disgust. Then he poked at it with one finger. Mr Grittysnit stared at the smear of soil the carrot left on his skin, and hurled it to a corner of the room.

'You've *soiled yourself*,' he hissed.

Then he came over to me.

He heaved and he wrenched. The pain was awful, but I bit my lips, determined not to make a fuss. After all that effort, he stepped away with just three blue petals in his hands. He stared at them, revolted. The veins on the side of his head throbbed as his eyes filled with realisation.

'They're real,' he said in a cold, flat voice.

A collective shriek rippled around the classroom. I sensed that everybody was itching to run over and see for themselves, but they stayed in their seats, one fearful eye on our headmaster, whose face was getting redder by the second.

'How dare you?' he bellowed. 'How dare you grow non-regulation heads in my school? They're not even grey! I've a fine mind to give you ten Bad Blots each for your appearance alone.'

I opened my mouth automatically, apologies ready to tumble out of my mouth as usual. But, to my horror, a peal of wild, uncontrollable laughter escaped instead.

Mr Grittysnit turned to stare at me, and I clamped my jaw shut to stop it from happening again.

Then Miss Mossheart gave a tiny yawn. It seemed to spread around the room like a Mexican wave.

'Beddy byes,' said Bella, slumping to the floor and lying down under her desk. 'And can someone do something about the light? It's too bright.'

'Yeah,' said Bertie, going pink at the sound of his own voice. 'Switch it off. I need darkness.'

'Darkness, darkness, darkness,' chanted our classmates, slowly sinking over their desks and putting their heads down.

Even Chrissie yawned as she delicately rested her head.

Mr Grittysnit opened his mouth to speak when the door to our classroom flew open.

Miss Balmforth, Mrs Harris and Mr Rayner from Years One, Three and Four ran in, faces creased with worry. Their eyes widened as they took in mine and Neena's appearance, but within seconds they turned back to our headmaster, wringing their hands and cringing with fear.

'What?' snapped Mr Grittysnit.

'It's . . . our classes, sir. We can't keep the children awake. They're all demanding a nap.'

CHAPTER 29

THE NEXT HOUR was a chaotic muddle of sleeping children being shaken awake, alarmed teachers huddling in groups around the school and the sound of Mr Grittysnit repeatedly roaring, 'WAKE UP!' into every afflicted classroom.

When he barged back into the Laminators to tell us that the entire school was dismissed for the day so we could shake off this lurgy, everyone gave sleepy cheers of delight.

'I'm going to go straight back to bed,' said Elka, shrugging her jacket on.

'Me too,' said Bertie, standing dazedly in the middle of the room.

'Your parents have all been called and will collect you from the school gates,' said Miss Mossheart through a huge yawn. 'Chrissie, your butler will collect you – both your parents are busy. Oh, and, Sorrel, the school office can't get hold of your mum at the factory or at home.'

'That's right! I totally forgot to give you a note from my mum this morning. Sorrel's mum is on a training day today so Sorrel's coming back with me – do you want to see the note?' said Neena smoothly, patting her pockets, while I looked at her in confusion.

Mum hadn't said anything about a training day. Had Neena's allotment messed with her brain?

Miss Mossheart had closed her eyes again and was swaying by her desk.

Neena pushed me gently towards the door. 'I've got an idea. Just go along with it.'

'Right. Er, see you tomorrow, Miss Mossheart! Just off to Neena's house now, like she said. Hope you feel better!'

Miss Mossheart gave a tiny snore in reply.

As we navigated our way through the crowds of children outside waiting to be collected, a gust of wind raced through the crowd, making everybody's hair ripple. I thought I could see little black things fly from head to head.

But when I rubbed my eyes and peered again, I saw nothing.

I braced myself for the stares and laughs as the crowd of parents and children took in my head and

Neena's. Fortunately, as worried parents huddled over their offspring with concern, we slipped easily past the throng. Even those who did notice our heads shrugged and looked away, as if they thought it was all part of some wacky school project and couldn't possibly be real.

Still, I felt horribly uneasy. What did Miss Mossheart mean, no one had been able to get in touch with Mum? Mum *always* kept her mobile in her overalls pocket, just in case the school ever needed to reach her. *And* her bedroom door had been shut when I'd left the house that morning, and she *always* left it open. So what was going on?

To make matters worse, I felt oddly vulnerable and strange in the open air. My sprouting head felt exposed and tingly. I could feel the flowers and grass on my scalp opening and swaying in the breeze as the wind danced through each stalk and blade, and it was as if all the nerve endings in my head were being tickled.

Basically, there were *way* too many sensations going on for me to handle all at once. I sighed with despair.

Neena gave my hand a firm squeeze and said, 'I've got a plan.'

Relief flooded through me.

'Guess where we're going,' she said.

'The doctor's?' I tried hopefully. 'Or to see someone with a chainsaw?'

She shot me a steady look. 'Strangeways, of course.'

'What? Our heads have erupted and you want to pay a visit to a garden centre?'

She nodded. 'You promised you'd show Sid if we grew anything, remember? Maybe he'll know what's going on.'

*

Fifteen minutes later, having been stared at by five dog walkers, one dad pushing a pram and a little old lady, it was actually a relief to push through the tunnel of weeds and stand in the cool green shade of Strangeways.

Florence found us first. Her tail wagged as she shuffled over to greet us.

But when she noticed the stalks and tendrils bobbing about on our heads, she bent her forelegs and gave a low growl. I stooped down and reached out to her, but she backed away, right into a pair of legs clad in faded green overalls.

'The seeds grew then,' said Sid quietly.

I straightened up and looked right at him, expecting him to gasp with shock, but to my surprise he did none of those things. He simply looked at our heads as a strange mixture of pride, fear and sadness flickered over his face.

The sound of the leaves rustling around us grew louder, like the roar of somebody growing impatient.

Sid nodded, as if to himself. 'This needs biscuits,' he said, turning round abruptly and walking back inside.

Neena and I looked at each other.

I shrugged and followed him. He obviously had something to say. Plus, you know, biscuits.

'This way,' Sid said, weaving a path to the back of the shop.

We stumbled about in the gloom until we got used to it, then followed him through a maze of dark, damp storerooms until we found ourselves in a small kitchen. On the shelves, green plants in pots crept and wound themselves round battered enamel mugs, plates and tins of food.

'Take a seat,' he urged, pointing to the wooden chairs grouped round the kitchen table.

Florence wandered over to a wicker basket in the corner, making sure to give us a wide berth as she went.

As Sid bustled about, heating milk in a pan, I noticed his hands were trembling.

Neena raised her eyebrows at me.

I raised my daisy stalks back.

He put three mugs of hot chocolate and a huge plate of custard creams down on the table with a heavy thump.

In a voice that shook with tiredness, as if it had been carrying secrets for too long, he said, 'It's time you knew the truth about this place.'

CHAPTER 30

'ROUGHLY THREE HUNDRED years ago,' Sid began, 'Little Sterilis wasn't a town at all. It was countryside, green and wild. There was a river, acres of wild wood, some meadows and one tiny hamlet called Little Cherrybliss, made up of three or four cottages.'

Little Cherrybliss? Where have I heard that name before?

'It all belonged to my ancestors, the Strangeways. And their lives have mostly faded away into the earth like old leaves. But my great-great-great-grandmother, Agatha Strangeways, is the one whose story matters here.'

He took a gulp from his mug with an unsteady hand. 'Now, the Strangeways were known to have green fingers.'

Neena laughed.

'Oh, I don't mean they were aliens or anything like that. No, that's what we call people with a knack for growing things. The Strangeways folk might have led simple lives, but they had a *gift* when it came to nature. They could grow what they wanted, when they wanted it.'

He gazed into the distance, and I knew he wasn't looking at the jam jars and cereal boxes on his shelves. He was looking at the past somehow, with his sad eyes. It was the same look I'd seen on Mum's face when she talked about the last time she'd danced in the rain. What *was* it about the past that made the grown-ups in my town look that way? As if it was a broken toy they couldn't fix?

Sid sighed, bringing me back to the present. 'Now, the Strangeways didn't need any of your supermarkets or takeaways. They lived off the vegetables and fruit they grew on the land. And they were so good at growing things, people often wondered if the soil was magic, or they were.'

'Were they?' I gasped, nearly choking on my second custard cream.

'Maybe,' said Sid, a small smile on his face. 'Or perhaps it was just good soil, and they knew how to tend it. If you love something properly, you can always make it flourish. Either way, the land meant everything to the Strangeways. They wanted for nothing. They had trees for their children to play in, and to shade them in summer. They had a river to swim in. Their homes were sweet with flowers, and they ate like kings. Life was good for them.'

Sid broke off and took another gulp from his mug.

Florence gave us a mournful look from her basket.

'Now, one little Strangeways girl was more skilled at growing things than the rest of them put together. Her name was Agatha Strangeways.' Sid looked at me, blinking fast. 'You have her trowel.'

Too right I had it. That old rusty trowel had made the Surprising Seeds come alive. A shiver ran down my neck.

'From the moment Aggie could walk, she spent all day roaming the meadows and swimming in the river. She could name every flower, plant and tree in field and valley by the time she was six. She loved every inch of Little Cherrybliss, and it loved her right back – you could tell, just by the way it grew green and lush when she was around it. She was rich with love for it, and it seemed to do her bidding. When she planted fruit trees, the fruit that grew was sweeter than anything anyone had tasted. The roses around her cottage bloomed all year long, never fading, never dying.

Folk started to say that she could make *anything* grow dreckley just by looking at it.'

Sid's voice wavered. He nibbled at a biscuit and was quiet a moment. 'Now, when she grew older, Aggie would load a cart up with what she'd grown, and take the veg, fruit and flowers into town to sell at the market. That was where she attracted the attention of a local businessman. He'd heard about this magical Strangeways land, and he wondered whether it could make him rich too.'

Sid glared at his mug as if he wanted to punch it. 'But he were after riches of a different sort.'

I hadn't seen Sid so angry since we'd first turned up at Strangeways and he'd waggled some secateurs in our faces.

He took a deep breath. 'Anyways, this fella kept asking to buy her land, but she kept turning him down. Once he caught on that she would never sell to him, things grew hard for Granny Aggie,' said Sid, his face hardening. 'It was said she lost her magic touch. There were droughts. Infestations of bugs and diseases killed her crops, although she could never discover how. The earth grew blighted and sick. The fish died in the river, and everything on the stalk was withered and twisted.

With no food to eat, Agatha and her children began to starve. Eventually, she had no choice but to do a deal with the businessman. In 1845 she sold him Little Cherrybliss – every last acre of it. An' he haggled her right down on the price once he saw how desperate she was.'

Sid's jaw was tight.

'Even then, Aggie tried to do right by it. She sold the land on the condition he would leave the river and the wood and the fields of wild flowers untouched. She sold it on the condition there still would be rich brown soil for people to grow vegetables in, and wide green spaces for children to explore. The businessman *said* he'd do all those things. He promised Little Cherrybliss would be a green town that lived "side by side with wild things". He swore he'd only build a few houses and leave her meadows and river untouched for future children to enjoy.'

I frowned. 'So where are they, then? Where are all these spaces? All we have is one run-down playground.'

'And that's on concrete,' added Neena.

Sid looked at us grimly. 'They're nowhere, girls,' he lied. It was all a mucky parcel of old rubbish. It was him that poisoned her land so her crops wouldn't grow.

He did that to make her desperate enough to sell the land to him. And he never had any intention of keeping Little Cherrybliss green and lovely. Not ever. He even changed its name to Little Sterilis, because he wanted to make it totally lifeless. The only thing he wanted to grow was his bank balance.'

'He sounds nasty,' said Neena. 'What was his name?'

Sid took a deep breath, and spat out one word. 'Valentini.'

My mind spun. 'But . . . that's Chrissie's surname. Are you talking about her family?'

Sid sighed. 'I don't know who this Chrissie is, but I'll wager she's related to the businessman who conned Granny Aggie, Julius Valentini. He died richer than ever, and he handed his property business to his lad, who handed it to his lad, and so on. It's run now by Rufus Valentini – or Ruthless, as I call him.'

'That's Chrissie's father! He's about to pour concrete over our playing field at school,' said Neena, staring at me.

I decided to look at my fingernails.

'Sounds about right.' Sid glowered. 'He's always lookin' to make money outta what's left of Little Cherrybliss. It's his family tradition, you could say.

When things got a bit tight for me moneywise, because I had no customers, he found out somehow, and now he won't leave me alone. He's desperate to buy up the last of the Strangeways land. That's why he sends over his heavies to intimidate me into selling. I call 'em the Valentini Villains.'

'You thought we were them, the first time we came!' I said, remembering.

Go on, leave, before I give you a little deadheading *you won't forget.*

'Yeah, well, eyesight's not what it used to be,' grumbled Sid. 'And for a time, they were my only visitors – until you came along, that is.' A small smile stole across his wrinkles, transforming him for a moment. 'Ruthless is desperate to get his hands on this land so he can build another shopping centre over it. But I can't let that happen. This place was the last thing Granny Aggie tried to do for Little Cherrybliss, before she died of a broken heart.'

'You mean she carried on living here?' asked Neena.

Sid nodded sadly. 'Oh yeah – she couldn't bear to leave it. She stayed in her little cottage to the end, and set up Strangeways as a gardening school. She tried to teach folk what she knew, but no one cared.

That conman didn't just poison the land – he poisoned folk against her. She never gave up, though. Almost to the end, Aggie tried to give away free plants, hoping the folk of the town would rise up and rebel against everything Valentini stood for. But they never did.'

Florence whined softly.

'It broke her heart to see the land paved over and smothered in concrete. To see her beloved trees and meadows ripped up and turned into factories and shops. There was nowhere to roam. There was nowhere green. It drove her mad with grief.'

'Poor woman,' I whispered. And suddenly I realised, with a jolt of recognition, that I'd heard a version of this story already. That voice I'd heard in Neena's shed at the weekend – it had been *Agatha*. My heart beat a little faster and I shuddered. I'd been hearing a ghost! *Spooky*.

'Neena,' I murmured. 'I've just worked out whose voice I heard in your shed.'

She raised her eyebrows. 'Whose?' she gasped.

'Agatha's.' My mind whirred, trying to remember. 'She said something like:

"He told me this, and he told me that,

But he lied to me, and he broke our pact.

And now I'm dead – alas, alack –
But with these seeds I'll get him back.'"

'Whoa,' said Neena.

'When I heard that, I'd thought she'd been talking about a broken heart. I thought she'd been abandoned by a true love and was hoping to be reunited with him. But Aggie hadn't wanted to get him back – she'd wanted *revenge*.'

Neena whistled softly.

Sid's voice grew quieter. 'By the end, she was reduced to wandering through the town, trying to give out bulbs and seeds to folk, with dead flowers and old twigs threaded through her hair. She became a figure of fun – and it turned people against growing stuff even more. They'd joke about it: "You'll end up potty as Potty Aggie if you do any *gardening*."'

He took a deep breath, and spoke in a rush, as if he had to before he lost his nerve. 'But I think all the jeering *did* make something grow after all – something mean and bitter. Inside her . . . Right before she died, she told her daughter, who subsequently told her son, who told his daughter, who told her daughter, who was my mother, who told me –' he gave a smile that was tinged with fear, but also something else –

'that on her deathbed Aggie had said she'd get her own back on the town that ignored her. That she'd make Little Cherrybliss grow again, in surprising ways. She said something about a wonderful revenge and . . . a packet of seeds. And then – right before she drew her last breath – she'd cackled and said, "*On their heads be it!*"'

We were silent for a few minutes as the full realisation of what he'd said sank in.

Anger beat hot punches inside my heart. 'So you're saying that these –' I flapped my hands furiously in the direction of the top of mine and Neena's heads – '*things* . . . are a curse?' I asked.

Sid gave a tiny nod.

The anger erupted inside me, thick and fierce. 'She tricked me! She never wanted to give me what *I* wanted – that was a lie to con me into sprinkling them and carrying out her revenge!'

I stared at my stupid, pale fingers, the ones that had unwillingly carried out her sick payback.

A loud, furious voice twisted its way out of my mouth. I turned on Sid to use it. 'Why didn't you *tell* us? Why didn't you warn us? If you'd known the Seeds were cursed with dark magic, you should have said!'

'But I weren't *sure* you had them,' Sid shouted back. 'You two were so secretive when you showed up. And I didn't want to ask too many questions in case I scared you off, and I'd never see you again. And I can't tell you how happy I was to see two children interested in growin' stuff . . . I felt as if, finally, this town could change for the better.'

His voice dropped to a low whisper, as if he was ashamed. 'And I was lonely. When you're lonely, you'll do anything for a bit of company, like not telling the whole truth – not all in one go anyway. I thought if I dumped all the facts on you at once it would be like putting too rich a compost on delicate seedlings; our friendship wouldn't survive.'

For a moment, the only sounds in the kitchen were of me breathing heavily, and Sid sniffling at the other side of the table.

'I've got to go,' I said bluntly.

And before Sid and Neena could say anything, I'd pushed my chair back and run for the door, heart slamming against my chest.

Because not only was I desperate to put as much distance between me and Sid as possible, but I'd suddenly realised something else.

Why Mum's bedroom door had been closed that morning.

Why Miss Mossheart hadn't been able to get in touch with her in the afternoon.

I ran all the way home.

CHAPTER 31

SLAM!

The front door crashed behind me.

I ran into the kitchen, calling for Mum. But she wasn't there. Or in the lounge. Or in the backyard, which, I noticed vaguely, had been totally concreted over once more. Vinnie must have finally succeeded somehow.

I stood in the hallway, panting heavily, and then I heard the sound of gentle sobbing coming from upstairs. I took the steps two at a time.

She was in her bedroom, staring at her reflection in the mirror. She was wearing her grubby yellow dressing gown, her eyes were wide and her face was pale in the darkness.

'Don't mind this,' she said in a strange tight voice, pointing at the little green tree which poked out proudly from the middle of her head. Her short blonde hair was dotted here and there with tiny daisies. 'I'm sure it's all a dream. Fancy some pancakes? How was school? Fancy some pancakes? How was sch—'

'Oh, Mum,' I said, sinking to my knees in the doorway. 'It's not a dream. I'm so—'

Sorry. '*I'm sorry*,' I was desperate to say. I knew I should tell her the truth: that I'd sprinkled the Seeds on her head because I'd been conned by a dead old woman with a grudge and a way with hypnotic rhyming sentences that were very persuasive. I wanted to lay my head in her soft lap and close my eyes and listen to her gently telling me that everything would be all right.

Yeah, right. Like that was going to happen. If I told her the truth, I'd just be one more problem she couldn't fix. *One more broken thing in our broken home.*

So I said nothing, and bent my head with shame.

She moved slowly over to me, reaching out to stroke the flowers on my head, and said, 'You too? But how has this happened?'

I took a deep breath and said, 'I don't know.'

Her eyes were moist. 'This isn't a dream, is it? It's real. I've been here all day – I couldn't go to work. I was so . . . desperate for light, and I never get any in the factory. All day long we're stuck inside this freezing room, and normally I can deal with that somehow, but today I just couldn't bear the thought of going in there for one second longer, and then I found myself dancing on the patio, laughing and speaking gibberish about fresh air and stuff, and then the pain started – like being bitten inside my scalp – and then this grew. And yours grew too. Oh, Sorrel. Don't worry, I'm going to call a doctor, and we'll get all this sorted.'

Mum was quiet for a while and then her hand flew up to her flushed cheek. 'What if it's a bug we caught from the house? It might be the mould spores in the bathroom – I've always worried about those . . .'

In the silence, the pipes moaned, the tap sobbed, the washing machine screeched through another cycle. Except they sounded more insistent than usual. Louder. A thought dropped into my brain like a pebble in a pond, clear and true.

'Mum,' I asked urgently, 'who owned this house, originally?'

She turned bewildered green eyes on me. 'You want to talk . . . about the *house*?'

I nodded.

She reached for her earring and fiddled with it absent-mindedly. 'I don't know, love. I do know it's one of the earliest cottages in the town – the estate agent was quite proud about that. All the paperwork's in the kitchen – you might find names in there.'

'In the messy kitchen drawer?' I asked.

She gave a dazed nod.

I flew downstairs.

*

I shook the yellowing plastic wallet of papers over the kitchen table. Official-looking letters, yellow Post-it notes and other bits and pieces fluttered out haphazardly.

Dear Ms Fallowfield, We are pleased to confirm the purchase of . . .

Dear Ms Fallowfield, We have done a survey of the property . . .

I groaned in frustration. Then I found a letter on a sheet of thick cream paper, with the words *GROLLIT AND BIGGINS SOLICITORS* across the top. Underneath the date were the words *Regarding the willow tree in the backyard.*

Bullseye.

As you may know, the official deeds of Cherry Cottage . . .

Cherry Cottage? Our house was *Cheery* Cottage . . . wasn't it?

. . . require, by law, complete protection of the willow tree in the backyard. It will not be removed, harmed or tampered with in any way, as requested by our client, Ms A. Strangeways, now deceased, in 1887.

Below this was my mum's signature in a jaunty bold writing I didn't recognise.

I sat there, staring at the paperwork, proof in my hand. No wonder I'd found the Surprising Seeds in the backyard. No wonder the house felt stuffed with grief and rage. No wonder the pipes and the telly and the clock sulked and moaned. No wonder the plastic fern got in on the act.

It was Agatha's *home*. It had been here when Little Cherrybliss was just a collection of three or four cottages, surrounded by fields and rivers and nature. She'd stayed here till her death, watching helplessly as she lost the world she'd loved.

I remembered the picture on the book in the library, *The Terrible Sad History of Little Cherrybliss*. That picture of the white cottage surrounded by a meadow? It had looked familiar because it was *my home*, even though it was grey, not white, now.

And the toxic gas of Agatha's anguish had seeped into this house and everything in it, hour by hour, day by day. Julius Valentini had bought Little Cherrybliss in 1845 . . . which meant the cottage had been soaking up Agatha's heartbreak for 174 years.

That was a lot of mood to take.

But what I couldn't understand was why the house was *still* moaning and groaning. Hadn't she got her revenge already?

I glanced out of the kitchen window at the hideous willow tree, and a shiver of recognition ran through me. It must have been hers. She'd planted it, and buried the Surprising Seeds underneath it. On cue, its branches rustled again, as if it was trying to . . . beckon me over. It looked like it was *waving*.

I stayed right where I was. There was no way I was going near it ever again. Who knew what nasty prank it would try next time? Turn my hands into twigs? I'd learned my lesson, thank you very much. I wasn't going to go out there for the rest of my life.

The fridge whined.

'Oh, shut up,' I said.

CHAPTER 32

'ARE YOU SICK?'

'No.'

'Are you experiencing double vision, light-headedness, headaches or swollen ankles?'

'No.'

'Can you tell me your full name, and the name of your school?'

'Sorrel Coriander Fallowfield, Grittysnits.'

After an hour of repeatedly dialling the doctor's number and getting a busy tone, Mum had managed to book the last two appointments of the day. She'd driven us there and then made us run inside with sheets over our heads, so people wouldn't stare.

'Just had our hair done,' Mum had said lightly to the receptionist at the front desk. 'Don't want it getting damp.'

Eventually, we'd been ushered into the doctor's consultation room.

Dr Stewart had said nothing for a solid three minutes, and simply stared. Then she'd recovered enough to stick stethoscopes on our chests and poke lights into our ears.

After ten minutes of alternately poking and prodding us and saying 'Fascinating, fascinating' a few hundred times, she sat back in her chair and made a baffled face.

'Well, if neither of you is actually *ill*, all we can do is hope that this . . . temporary growth dies down within a few days. If it doesn't, I can prescribe some antibiotics, which might kill it off,' she said, typing rapidly into her computer. 'Sorry for the yawning – it's been the strangest afternoon. Loads of kids are coming in complaining of sleepiness. Haven't had a moment's rest . . .'

I zoned out. It was hard to think in the stuffy room and I started fidgeting, irritated thoughts running through my brain.

Why were all the doctor's windows shut?

In fact, come to think of it, why were none of the windows open in the entire surgery?

And why did everyone look so miserable and tired today? Even all the grown-ups did, I realised. Mum, the receptionist in the waiting room, Miss Mossheart,

Neena's parents – and the stressed-out doctor . . .

A bald man in a white tunic poked his head round the door.

'Ah, yes, come in, please, Nurse Barker,' said our doctor. 'Shut the door as quickly as you can, thank you.'

The nurse stared at me and Mum as politely as he could. 'Hello,' he said gently. 'I pull out septic toenails and splinters all the time – I'm sure these growths aren't that different. We'll have you right in a jiffy.'

And they did try hard, I'll give them that. They tried tweezers, they tried forceps, they even tied bits of string round the flowers poking out of my scalp and attached them to the door handle before slamming the door to see if that would uproot my flowers. No dice.

By 7.00 p.m., as the sound of the cleaner's Hoover outside the room got louder, they admitted defeat.

'We've never seen anything like this before, love,' said Nurse Barker.

'I think, until we find a cure that works, the best thing for you is to stick to your normal life,' said Dr Stewart, cocking her silver bob to one side. 'Keep things as ordinary as possible. Nothing like a dose of routine to make us feel better, eh?'

Mum nodded slowly.

'At least you've got a sensible one there, Miss Fallowfield. If anyone can handle this sort of sickness, it's a nice quiet child who doesn't panic.'

'Oh yes,' said Mum, smiling as she rubbed my hand. 'She's never given me a moment's worry, this one. Good as gold.'

I smiled shakily.

And then I took a deep breath and . . .

. . . exhaled in a long, meaningful, confessional way.

As far as completely wordless admissions of guilt go, it was spectacular.

Unfortunately, Mum completely ignored it. But I want it on the record that I did try to come clean before things spiralled completely out of control. Yep, if there was an award for Trying To Tell The Truth In A Totally Silent Way Through The Medium Of Sighing, I'd have won it. No contest. Total shoo-in.

CHAPTER 33

I RAN TO my bedroom mirror as soon as I woke up the next morning.

Mossy forehead – check.

Daisy-stalk eyebrows – check.

A massive clump of flowers and grass where my hair had previously been – check.

So that was *great*.

My reflection upset me so much, I knew that if I stared at it for too much longer, I'd start to cry. And if I started, I wasn't sure I'd be able to stop. And then I'd be the grassy-haired girl who couldn't stop crying, and I could do without that extra complication. So I jerked myself away from the hideous apparition, dressed hurriedly and ran downstairs.

On the hallway table, a note lay propped up against the dying plastic fern.

Gone to work, with a massive hat! Stay
brave – I'm sure they'll die down today.
Mum xxx

Neena's special tap rang through the hallway. I
shuffled to the door and opened it.

She squinted at me and tilted her head to one side.
'Why did you run off yesterday?'

'I had to get home. It's Mum – she's sprouted too.'

'What? Why? How could she have? You only
sprinkled the Seeds on *us*, didn't you?'

I gave a tiny shake of my head, not in the mood
to recount what had happened in the kitchen and the
voices I'd heard. Neena's eyes were full of questions,
but, to my relief, she must have sensed I didn't want to
explain.

'Okay. Well, thanks to your grumpiness, I had
to spend a couple of hours consoling Sid, who was
miserable after you left and kept apologising for his
ancestors and generally being alive. Then I went home,
which wasn't much better. When they saw my head,
Mum fainted, and Dad shouted and raved and blamed
my chemistry sets. He even—' She blinked and rubbed
her eyes. 'Anyway, never mind. Then I had the worst

night's sleep of my life. Slugs kept crawling all over my face, trying to get near my crops. I spent eight hours trying to fight them off but as soon as I closed my eyes, they'd appear again.'

I nearly laughed, but then a terrible thought struck me. 'You didn't tell your parents about the Surprising Seeds, did you? Or that I sprinkled them on our heads?'

'Course not,' said Neena, her scalp tomatoes wobbling slightly as she shook her head. 'But I don't think they'd have taken it in anyway. Look at her.'

I peered past Neena to her mum, standing on my doorstep. Mrs Gupta was staring fixedly at my face, her eyes rigid and wide. Her eyelids twitched just once with a tiny flick upwards, but then she widened her eyeballs again. Her smile looked as painted as the ones on my Lego toys.

'Shock,' whispered Neena.

We walked the rest of the way to school in silence, to the accompaniment of stares from passers-by. My mind felt flappier than a cat flap in a hurricane, through which questions flew like a flurry of frightened kittens.

Would Mum be okay at work? Why had she looked so disappointed when Dr Stewart had told us to stick to our daily routines? Did I have even a hope of winning the Grittysnit Star competition any more?

And *why* was there such a massive queue of kids outside the water fountain at 8.55 a.m. in the morning?

CHAPTER 34

IN OUR CLASSROOM that morning, things became increasingly surprising.

Bella kept rubbing her head and asking to rest in a damp dark place.

Robbie filched a box of chalk from the art supply cupboard and ate the entire packet at his desk. When he finished, he had multicoloured teeth.

Bertie was glued to the window, staring out towards the damp grey concrete playground, sighing and looking longingly at an old wall as if it was an entire box of sticky doughnuts.

Elka kept asking to go and stick her head in the sandpit.

Even Miss Mossheart seemed restless. She didn't seem to particularly care that Robbie was eating chalk at his desk, or Bertie was staring out of the window, or that Bella was lying down under her desk with a cardigan on top of her face, moaning. She just kept staring at a fly that was buzzing against our window. While licking her lips.

Neena also seemed distracted, rustling around in her rucksack and fidgeting in her chair.

'What's up with you?' I said, as soon as the bell rang for break.

'I'm looking for my petition to save the playing field,' she admitted. 'I think I need to give it another shot; see if I can persuade more people to sign today. It takes a while for injustice to sink in sometimes.'

'But the scaffolding's up. The grass is gone. It's as good as built, Neena. You might as well give up,' I said.

'You're wrong, Sorrel,' said Neena. 'The fight's only over when you think it's over.' And she grabbed her clipboard and ran for the door.

*

I sat at our desk, listless and unhappy, and tugged viciously at the flowers sticking out of my head. The undercurrent of strangeness running through the morning, not to mention my head, had left me unsettled and disturbed. I felt as if I was losing, bit by bit, the things most important to me: my status, my normality, not to mention my hair. It was as if life's greasy fingers had gone through my pockets and left nothing valuable behind. I felt tainted, greasy and ashamed of what was left.

My eye fell on the Obedience Point chart on the wall. Chrissie was in the lead, with one – and both Neena and I were lagging behind with one Bad Blot each. I stared glumly at them for a while, my hopes for the future fading away as clearly as if someone had doused them with corrosive bleach.

I hated the bare patch on my jumper where my Head of Year badge had once been. I hated knowing that Chrissie would be flying to Portugal on *my* holiday. Like she even needed to anyway; the Valentini family had a private jet and holiday homes in practically every continent. It wasn't fair.

All this stuff about Agatha and Sid and what the Valentinis had done to the Strangeways and Little Cherrybliss back in the murky past . . . did it really matter? What's done was done. It was ancient history. I couldn't *do* anything about it, anyway.

What was *much* more important was how I was going to make my way back into Mr Grittysnit's good books, and I wasn't going to do that by wasting any more time worrying about old stories, old people, old grudges and feuds that didn't concern me. I had a reputation to restore!

I caught sight of Neena wandering around the yard with her clipboard and a thought occurred to me.

And in the overheated oven of my mind, a twisted idea began to rise like a nasty cake.

I got up quickly and scuttled out of my classroom.

CHAPTER 35

I HURRIED DOWN the corridor to Mr Grittysnit's office and tapped on his door.

'Enter,' he barked.

I twisted the handle and walked inside his lair.

He stared at me from behind his desk and frowned.

'Head still sprouting?'

'Yes, sir. Sorry, sir.'

'You should be sorry, Sorry.'

I blinked back tears.

'What do you want, girl?'

I took a deep breath, and forced myself to speak.

'Neena Gupta is outside . . . tryingtostoptheexamhall sir,' I gasped.

His eyes narrowed. He sat back in his chair, and stared at me for a while.

'Explain.'

I took a deep breath. I was too far in it to back out now. My throat felt as if it was coated with stinging nettles. 'She's trying to gather signatures against your exam hall, sir. She's out there right now.'

A horrible silence filled the room.

And then, hating myself a bit, I whispered, 'Can I have an Obedience Point please, sir?'

He nodded, black eyes gleaming. 'I'll have it arranged immediately,' he said. 'Turns out you're not so bad after all, Sorry. You're back in the game. Congratulations.'

'Thanks. Are you going to . . . Are you going to punish her? I don't want her to be expelled or anything—'

'Not right away,' said Mr Grittysnit. 'Sometimes I like to sit on useful information until I know how best to utilise it.'

He smiled, and it reminded me of that time I went on a ghost train in Weston-super-Mare and a mechanical zombie jumped out and made me wet myself.

I stammered my thanks, shut his door behind me and walked down the corridor as fast as I could.

I'd become a human snow globe. Silver shards of glittery pride and ambition tumbled around inside me. They looked pretty, but they felt like splinters of glass when they landed.

I shook my head, grinding to a halt on the carpet as I puzzled over things. I'd done what I had to do. I'd been good. So why did it feel so bad?

I crossed my fingers, hoping he would only punish Neena with another Bad Blot, as she didn't seem to particularly mind those. Perhaps she'd see them as a badge of honour, in which case I'd probably done her a favour.

Yeah. That's right. Done her a favour. You're all give, give, give, Sorrel.

I went into the classroom and sat quietly at my desk, waiting for the school bell to ring. Puking felt likely and I couldn't stop shivering.

Then, when Miss Mossheart walked in, I saw the Obedience Point in her hand and I felt it hard to meet her eyes.

She put it up next to my name on the chart, her 'congratulations' sounding strangely muted.

A short time later, everyone else came in from outside, yawning and scratching their heads, and when their eyes sidled over to the chart and they saw the cardboard star next to my name, I felt a strange mixture of shame and pride.

Only Neena looked at me head-on, as she sat down at our desk. 'And how exactly did you get that, Sorrel?'

'It doesn't matter,' I said quickly.

'Oh, I think it does,' she said heavily. 'I think it matters a lot.'

*

After the lunch break, Mrs Pinch appeared at our classroom door. I was glad of the distraction. Her eyes were sparkling and her lips were painted with fresh red lipstick.

'I have news,' she announced in a bright voice.

'Yes?' said Miss Mossheart.

'There's a journalist from the *Sterilis Standard* hanging around by the school gates,' she said. 'He's heard there's a mysterious bug going around the school. You need to remain in your classrooms on total lockdown – it would be a disaster for our reputation if he found out about Neena and Sorrel.'

My neck went floppy again, but this time with humiliation.

'I'm going to go outside and deal with him,' said Mrs Pinch, and off she went.

Through the classroom window I saw her strutting to the school gates like a model on a catwalk. At one point she even flicked her hair. In fact, she seemed to be taking her time telling this journalist to go away.

The man smiled and nodded at whatever she was

saying but stayed right where he was. I noticed Mrs Pinch throw her head back and give a peal of laughter.

'Okay, class, let's try to concentrate on our multiple divisions, shall we?' said Miss Mossheart, giving out some exercise sheets.

As we began to read the words in front of us, a screech of tyres pierced the air.

A large white van with the words NATIONAL SCOOPS had driven on to the pavement outside our school. Its double door slid open and four excited-looking adults climbed out, clutching huge cameras, big furry sticks and microphones. They gathered on the pavement next to the first journalist.

The last adult out of the van was a blond man in an extremely tight blue suit. As soon as he swaggered on to the pavement, a woman began touching his face with a powder puff while a teenager in a black hoodie brought him a cup of coffee.

Then the whole lot of them turned and started to look hungrily through the school gates.

CHAPTER 36

By now, we'd all given up any pretence of caring about multiple divisions and had crowded round our window to observe the scene. The man in the tight blue suit was gargling with water.

Soon we spotted Mr Grittysnit running up to the gates. He started to wave his arms about and shout.

'Open the windows,' said Miss Mossheart in a new, strangely firm voice, 'so we can hear what's going on.'

Elka pushed out our windows as wide as she could.

Mr Grittysnit's furious voice could now be heard loud and clear. 'You're on school property – clear off!'

Blue-suit Man said something too quiet for us to hear, but the smile never left his face.

A ripple of interest began to spread through our crowd at the window. Something unusual was happening to Mrs Pinch. She'd started staggering around on the tarmac, just a few steps away from the gates, clutching her head.

Mr Grittysnit didn't seem to notice, as he was still shouting at Blue-suit, but the other grown-ups from the National Scoops van began to nudge each other. One woman very slowly aimed her camera at Mrs Pinch.

'What do you mean, in the public interest?' Mr Grittysnit bellowed. 'This is *my* school – it has nothing to do with the public. You're trespassing, and I demand that you leave before I call the—'

The shout from Mrs Pinch must have reached him, because he stopped talking and looked over sharply at his secretary, who was doubled over as if in pain.

What she said next turned my blood cold. 'Argh! Bees! Head! Hurt!'

A green bush tipped with bright purple flowers was rapidly bursting out of the middle of her scalp. It started off small, but within a minute or two it had grown until it was bigger than her actual head. A cloud of white butterflies appeared and hovered in the air just above her head, as if drawn to her plant. Then, all at once, they floated downwards in a fluttering mass. Within moments, her head was covered in hundreds of shimmering insects. Her face could not be seen at all.

'Help me!'

Her muffled cry, smothered by a layer of butterfly wings, sounded desperate. Every time she tried to swat them away, the butterflies paused in the air for a minute before flying back down again.

Outside the school gates, the cameras flashed.

Mrs Pinch staggered around, her arms outstretched.

One of the men talked into his mobile. 'Send everyone you've got,' his excited voice rang out. 'This is the scoop of the century!'

Blue-suit Man turned to the largest film camera and began to speak into it. He had a funny sort of look on his face, as if he'd just walked into his lounge on Christmas Day and found an entire roomful of presents with his name on.

Meanwhile, Mrs Pinch lurched blindly about. After a moment, Mr Grittysnit grabbed her hand with distaste and dragged her back inside the school, shooting her disgusted looks all the way, as the cameras behind them continued to flash and film.

Once more, a terrible shriek of pain pierced the air. But this one came from the desk behind me.

We all turned and stared at Bella.

Fear drenched me like an icy waterfall.

She clutched her head, her brow a tapestry of worried lines, as she moaned with shock. 'Oh, stop it! Someone, please stop it!' Bella said.

She shot Chrissie a pleading look, but Chrissie simply sat and stared in horror at the cluster of orange knobbly mushrooms beginning to poke out of Bella's blonde hair.

The bigger they grew, the smellier they got. Within five minutes, the stench of unwashed feet was overpowering and we all began to clutch our noses.

'Yuck,' said Chrissie finally, her narrow face wrinkled up. 'You've grown a toadstool head.' She pinched her nose with her hand and inched her chair away.

Bella sobbed.

'Actually, Chrissie, you're wrong there. It may look like a toadstool, but it's technically a mushroom. Your friend is sporting a *Pseudocolus fusiformis*, most commonly known as a stinkhorn,' said Miss Mossheart, looking more confident and alert than I'd ever seen her.

'Ew, you're fungus,' said Chrissie. 'Forget it, Pearlman.

You're on your own now – until you decide to be *normal* again. I can't risk my health or my school reputation by sitting next to that. I *am* Head of Year, after all,' she said, shooting me an evil grin. Then she got up and began to move towards the door.

Bella looked at her desk so sadly that even I felt sorry for her.

'Chrissie, get back to your desk *immediately*,' snapped Miss Mossheart. It was the loudest I'd ever heard her speak.

Chrissie looked back, surprised. 'I'm going to tell Daddy you've told me off,' she said in a voice a little less confident than usual.

'Fine by me,' said Miss Mossheart in a voice that gave me goosebumps.

And then her eyes went wide, and she flinched.

Our classroom went as silent as a graveyard at midnight. We watched in awe as her wiry brown curls seemed to recede into her scalp, to be replaced by a clump of bright green leaves at the end of long, delicate tendrils snaking out of her head. At the end of each green leaf were two rows of sharp spikes. They looked a lot like teeth.

'Wow,' breathed Neena admiringly.

Miss Mossheart reached into her handbag and pulled out a small pocket mirror, which she held up to her face. She smiled with delight and then surveyed the entire classroom, her head held high.

'I see you're admiring my Venus flytrap,' said Miss Mossheart in her new firm voice. 'Beautiful, isn't she?'

Chrissie's green eyes got wider. She looked nervously around the classroom and took her hand off the doorknob.

'But she's very hungry,' said Miss Mossheart, staring at Chrissie.

In the silence that followed, I noticed two things:

1. **This was the first time I'd ever seen Chrissie look frightened.**
2. **There was a fly in the room.**

At first, its buzz was faint. Then, as if drawn by an invisible force, it landed on one of the bright green leaves waiting patiently on Miss Mossheart's head. The fly started to walk on its waxy, shiny surface as happily as if it was out for a summer stroll.

Miss Mossheart said softly, 'Oh yes, my little flytrap is very hungry. And she really doesn't like to be answered back. It makes her rather . . . snappy.'

Suddenly, the leaf blades on Miss Mossheart's head snapped shut on the fly. There was a sickening crunch. That poor old fly didn't stand a chance. Soon, all we could see was its death throes inside the leaf. Then they too were finished.

Chrissie gulped.

'So, you don't want to make her too cross, do you, my girl?' said Miss Mossheart in a voice like a vine looking for something to wrap round. Her eyes shone brightly as she stared at Chrissie.

The Venus flytrap rotated slowly in Chrissie's direction as if it was looking for her.

With a frightened shriek, Chrissie rushed back to her chair next to Bella.

A lovely smile played about Miss Mossheart's mouth. She held her head high and her eyes seemed to sparkle. The two pink spots of colour on her cheeks had deepened and the normal furrow of worry between her eyebrows had disappeared. The spiky leaf on top of her head gave out a tiny satisfied burp.

CHAPTER 37

Neena nudged me, her eyes wide. 'That's six people in total that have sprouted. How is this happening?' she whispered.

'I have no idea!' I replied. 'I didn't put it on anyone else's head apart from ours and Mum's! Honest!'

Then things got properly weird and freaky.

Over the next ten minutes, other heads in our classroom started sprouting too. We barely had time to finish gawping at one head before somebody else clutched theirs in agony. It was awful.

Aisha Atticus grew a patch of tall green flowers, at least half a metre tall, that ended in vivid purple flowers. Every time she moved, they got snagged on the light fixtures.

'Oooh, you've grown some *Verbena bonariensis*,' said Miss Mossheart, looking more animated than she'd looked in any of our lessons to date. 'Lovely little perennial.'

Robbie's head was covered in pale pink daisy-like flowers that tumbled over each other in a bright carpet of colour while he stared at his desk as if he was about to be sick.

'That's an African daisy, Robbie – they thrive on a chalky soil,' exclaimed Miss Mossheart delightedly.

Bertie grew some orange and yellow flowers out of his head.

'Wallflowers,' Miss Mossheart said.

Little grey stones and tiny daisies popped out all over Elka's head.

'A rockery,' said Miss Mossheart admiringly. 'Very low maintenance.'

Polly Minkle had tumbling sea-green stalks with tiny round green leaves that cascaded all the way down to her neck.

'String of pearls, a lovely houseplant,' uttered Miss Mossheart, touching them approvingly. 'Oh, well done, class, you *are* doing well.'

And so it went on.

Those that hadn't sprouted were cowering visibly from those that had.

Meanwhile, the worrying, telltale sounds of pained shrieks and gasps from other classrooms began to get louder. Children weren't just sprouting in our class – it was happening all over the school.

Panicked teachers were running around the school, fragments of their conversations reaching us from the corridor.

'All of our Reception kids are gazing out of the window.'

'The catering staff are all complaining about bee stings . . .'

'A girl from Year Three was caught sunbathing on the roof!'

'. . . drinking dirty paint water like it was squash.'

'There's a whole class of Year Twos demanding to be let outside so they can lie down in the mud . . .'

And outside the school gates, the scrum grew. More camera crews and journalists arrived. Vans, cars and motorbikes piled up haphazardly on the pavements outside the school, blocking the road and making other drivers beep their horns in frustration. Men and women in white coats and stethoscopes had also appeared and were walking about purposefully, talking to the journalists and shouting for Mr Grittysnit to release the children so they could be treated.

Soon, the throng was thickened by wild-eyed

parents, screaming for their children and demanding answers.

The telephone on Miss Mossheart's desk rang. She picked it up, said hello, listened to the barking voice coming out of it for two seconds and put the receiver down again.

'School dismissed,' she said.

We filed out into the crowded playground. Each time a fresh batch of children appeared, the journalists would grin, the scientists would frown and the parents would shriek. It was like they were watching a firework display.

There were children with ferns, children with long golden grasses, children with small decorative bushes growing out of their heads. There were children whose heads were covered with spiky cacti and children with bees buzzing happily among their flower stalks.

Anyone could see plainly that the school now consisted of two types of kids: those with normal heads, and those whose heads were sprouting. As the latter slunk in shock through the playground towards their parents, the normal kids gave them a wide berth, throwing them fearful, fascinated glances, as if to say, 'Will I be next?' Best friends walked apart from each other. Sworn enemies marched together. The Surprising Seeds had thrown the normal order of things upside out and inside down.

Mr Grittysnit stalked across the yard with a bunch of keys and opened the gates. The afflicted children walked through them and into the crowd, past the journalists, who tried to grab them for interviews and thrust microphones into their faces.

'Can you tell us how you're feeling?'

'Can you just turn round a bit so we can film your whole head?'

'Are there any words you want to share with the public?'

As fast as the parents would push the journalists away, more would appear, who would then be shoved away in turn by the scientists and doctors, staring and prodding and asking if they could run some medical tests. A few scared children nodded meekly and went into ambulances with their equally frightened parents, but a lot shook their heads and headed straight for their family cars.

Neena and I stayed in the playground, too stunned to do more than watch.

'This is all your fault,' shouted a woman in an orange

Puffa jacket as she pointed a finger at Mr Grittysnit, then at the small girl beside her, whose head was covered in silvery grey-green cabbages. 'How do you explain this?'

Mr Grittysnit looked furious. 'This has nothing to do with me,' he snapped. '*I'm* the one that keeps all these children on the straight and narrow. It's you parents who've encouraged this epidemic, with your late bedtimes and cuddles and total lack of discipline—'

'Well, I think it's a hygiene problem,' another parent interrupted. 'You should have got everybody to wash their hands more thoroughly every five minutes—'

'*I* think it's the catering – you're obviously not feeding them properly.'

'I always knew that there was something strange in the milk at this school.'

'If my daughter gets this disease, I'm going to sue whichever child brought this bug into the school,' yelled a man in a green waxed jacket. 'And I'll bring a huge lawsuit against each and every parent too for not keeping their child at home, thereby spreading the filth.'

'What?' exploded a furious woman on his left.

He shrugged at her. 'If your George gives whatever

he's got to my Gertrude, I have every right to sue.'

'You'd better think twice about threatening me. Besides, maybe your Gertrude could do with a new hairstyle – when was the last time she brushed her hair?'

'How *dare* you judge her looks? I'll have you know she won the Little Sterilis Beautiful Baby competition when she was only nine months old.'

'Oh yeah? Was that the year the judges were *blind*?'

On and on and on they went.

The shouting got shoutier, the pointing got pointier and the scowls got scowlier. Younger children and babies started to cry, arrests were made, and the only people who were smiling were the journalists, who kept telling each other what an incredible story this was and asking if there was anywhere nearby they could get a decent skinny mocha.

My mind ran in exhausted laps, back to the beginning, to the end, to the beginning, to the end . . . I felt there was an answer to what was happening under my nose, but my mind was too frazzled to see it. I circled back to the beginning again. I pictured the packet of Seeds in my hands. The rattling. I remembered Neena reading the words on the back in a funny voice . . . *'Self-seeding be these seeds.'*

What does that mean? I don't know.

But, I realised suddenly, *someone* would know. I could just make out the green tendrils of her head, in fact. I grabbed Neena's hand and ran over to her.

'Hello, girls,' said Miss Mossheart. 'Your parents not here yet?'

'Actually, I had a question about, erm, gardening.' I dropped my voice to a whisper. 'And I know it's something you're an expert in.'

'Oh yes?' she said, her entire face lighting up. 'Fire away.'

'I was wondering if you could tell me what "self-seeding" means? I, erm, heard someone talking about it.'

Miss Mossheart frowned at me for a moment, then her brow cleared. 'Oh, well, that's quite simple. Basically, anything which self-seeds spreads itself.'

'Spreads itself? You mean like . . . a spread on toast? Or chocolate spread?'

She smiled. 'Not quite. Something which is self-seeding is a plant or flower which sows itself, with very little need for human intervention. Self-seeders only need a little gust of wind or something like that and they begin to spread and grow all over the place, often in nooks and crannies we never thought they'd be able to grow in.'

Miss Mossheart was smiling, oblivious to the fact she was telling us the worst news in the world. 'Clever little blighters, self-seeders. Once they self-seed, they begin a perpetual cycle of life. It's like a family, almost. Lots and lots of generations which spread themselves and never die out.'

'Never die out?' My voice came out as a cracked whisper. 'So, self-seeders will . . .'

'Grow for ever,' said Miss Mossheart, nodding.

I clutched Neena for support.

Finally, I understood the true scale of Agatha Strangeways's revenge on Little Sterilis, and it was more terrifying than I had ever imagined.

Because it would last for ever. I wobbled on my feet, picturing generation after generation of Little Sterilis children with slugs on their faces and grass for hair.

'Oh, dear Sorrel, you look exhausted. You must go home, give your head a good drink of water and get some rest. In the meantime, I'm going to stand by the kitchen bins and see if I can catch a little snack or two for my flytrap.' And she wandered off.

Neena and I stared at the assorted crowd shouting at each other in the car park.

Neena gulped. 'So Agatha Strangeways invented a

Seed that would be able to plant itself on every head in Little Sterilis?'

I nodded miserably. 'Do you remember that really windy day we had a few days ago? Did you see all those little black things flying about in the air? They weren't nits or dust. They were the Surprising Seeds spreading. And now it's only a matter of time before everybody in the town is infected. And if they find out who started it all . . .'

I looked at the shouting mob and gulped. If they were this angry now, what would they be like when they found out who did this to their little darlings?

I took a deep breath to steady my voice. 'Promise me you won't tell anyone.'

Neena nodded slowly. 'It's such a shame though,' she said. 'This is an incredible scientific discovery. For a packet of seeds buried such a long time ago to retain such power—'

'Promise.'

'Promise.' She paused. 'Is that your mum? Wow, what's she got? Is that a . . .'

'Yep,' I said flatly. 'It is.'

I caught sight of Mum's pale face under her green tree. Her eyes raked the crowd for me while also darting nervous glances at the journalists, who, like tigers sniffing the air for their next kill, had gone very quiet and very still.

'Come on,' I said to Neena. 'Let's go.'

I reached for her hand and walked towards the crowd, shrinking back imperceptibly from Mr Grittysnit as he stood guard at the gate, hoping he couldn't sense my guilty conscience.

Like a human-shaped jellyfish, the crowd surged and moved around me. My breath came in short, painful pants. I could smell sweat and coffee and a strange metallic smell, which made me shrink backwards. I also felt weirdly protective of the top of my head even though I still hated it, obviously. The weight of the crowd seemed to press in on me and I lost my grip on Neena's hand.

I kept my head down and tried to push through the crowd, but I tripped on my shoelace and stumbled. I spotted a large handbag and reached out to it for support, but the woman above it yanked it away from me as if she couldn't bear for me to touch it.

I fell to the ground. A wall of legs and shoving feet surrounded me. For a minute, I was really frightened. Perhaps the crowd would simply stamp me out.

Do they already know this is all my fault?

Then someone was pulling me up, and a pair of freezing arms smelling faintly of pepperoni wrapped themselves around me in a tight embrace.

Mum said, 'It's all right, darling, I've got you.'

I hugged her back just as tightly. 'Oh, Mum,' I said, but my words got swallowed up in my sobs.

'Yah. Sorry, Mum, but could you say that again, but just a bit louder for our viewers at home? Really touching moment,' said Blue-suit. 'But before the run-through, just wait a tick while my little miracle worker makes you a *teeny* bit more camera-friendly – I'm all for gritty authenticity, but we're trying to present the news here, not a horror film. Kiki? Kiki? We've got a severe case of BB here.'

'What are you talking about?' hissed Mum.

'Bags and blackheads,' said Blue-suit Man. 'Very common in the provinces – you mustn't blame yourself.'

CHAPTER 38

AFTER MUM HAD snarled a few *extremely* rude words at Blue-suit Man and threatened to do something completely unmentionable with Kiki's make-up brush unless we were released instantly from her clutches, she bundled me into our battered car.

It was a relief to sink into its back seat and shut the door on the shouting mob and the police. The last person I saw as we slowly drove away was Chrissie, standing right behind Mr Grittysnit in the school grounds, checking the gold watch round her wrist.

I fell into an exhausted silence.

Miss Mossheart's words played over and over in my mind. '*Grow for ever.*'

In the quiet of the car, I could see, even more clearly, the horrible brilliance of Agatha Strangeways's vengeance on the town that had betrayed her. All her Seeds had needed was to find someone stupid enough to sprinkle them.

Guilty as charged.

The Surprising Seeds would never stop spreading. Which meant that the heads of everybody in my entire town would eventually sprout. It had started already, and it was only a matter of time for the rest. We were doomed.

Even as we drove home, those heads would be self-seeding up and down the streets. Tomorrow, a fresh batch of heads would grow. It was like, literally, the worst game of dominoes. In just a matter of days, the entire population of Little Sterilis would be afflicted with the most monstrous epidemic the world had ever seen.

And what would happen then? What if Agatha's dark magic went a bit haywire and didn't just execute her revenge on her town? What if it moved from town to town, city to city? Would every person on the entire planet be walking around with a headful of cabbages and caterpillars?

Oh, and who would the entire world blame?

Me. That's who. People would spit at me in the streets. I'd be Public Enemy Number One. As for Mum – well, she'd be Public Enemy Number Two, just because she had unfortunately given birth to Public Enemy Number One.

Mum shot me a look in the rear-view mirror. 'How are you feeling, darling?' she said after a pause.

'Fine,' I sighed.

'Sure?' she said, her dark green eyes troubled.

'Yep. How are you?' I asked, to change the subject more than anything.

She took a deep breath and then she said, 'Well, I've been fired.'

*

We turned into our road while I tried to wrap my head around this latest disaster.

'What? How? Why? I thought you were brilliant at your job! I thought they couldn't possibly manage without you . . .'

Mum parked and rummaged around in her handbag for our house keys. 'Well, that's not completely true, sweetheart. Anyone can do my job, really. It's the machines that my bosses can't do without, not me. I was just a glorified tube cleaner. I pressed a few keys. It wasn't rocket science.'

We got out of the car and walked up to our front door.

Mum pushed it open, and I had the funny feeling she was reluctant to meet my eye. 'Mrs Grindstone said my tree made me look unprofessional and was against health and safety rules. Said things hadn't been working out for a while anyway. She didn't think I was giving a hundred and ten per cent to the job. Apparently, me constantly asking to use fresher ingredients in a frozen pizza factory isn't a good idea . . .'

We walked into our cold hallway.

'But you love working there! I mean, you have a badge and those cool overalls and . . .' My voice faltered at the sight of Mum's dark, unreadable eyes.

'I'll cope,' she said. 'I promise. Now, how about some squash and something to eat? I made some brownies at the weekend – you like those, don't you? Why don't you go and sit down and we'll have a little cuddle in front of the telly?'

I nodded, slightly cheered by the prospect of one of Mum's delicious home-made brownies, but then a terrible thought occurred to me: *Now I no longer have a free supply of Chillz Rejects.*

I slumped on the sofa, narrowly avoiding impaling myself on a sticky-out spring, flicked the telly on and consoled myself with the thought that at least things couldn't get any worse.

CHAPTER 39

I JABBED AT the buttons on the remote control, hoping to find something nice and soothing to watch, like a cartoon or an episode of Mum's favourite cookery programme, *Now You're Cooked*.

Unfortunately, the telly seemed to have other ideas. Every single channel was broadcasting a serious news programme. I flicked impatiently, but then I saw a face I recognised on the screen.

It was the blond man with the white teeth and the blue suit, the man from *National Scoops*. Behind him were the school gates of Grittysnits. At the bottom of the screen was a rolling red tab which said: *Worrying head-plant outbreak in small, otherwise unremarkable town.*

Mum put the plate of brownies on the coffee table and sank down next to me on the sofa. She reached for the remote and turned up the volume.

'. . . tensions here are high outside the Grittysnit School in Little Sterilis, where there seem to be more questions than answers about the source of this horrific outbreak.' The man's eyes twinkled but his face remained solemn. 'Previously, Little Sterilis was an ordinary – some might say humdrum – town, known for nothing more than producing the cheapest frozen pizzas in Britain.'

Mum gave a snort.

'But since ten o'clock this morning, it's become the most famous town in the country. This epidemic is the first of its kind in history. But the people around me, rightly, don't feel like celebrating their newfound fame. Angry locals demanding the truth are gathering behind me, and still nobody seems to know—'

The telly suddenly went silent.

I got up and gave it a bit of the old Whack and Pray.

'. . . while the cause of the outbreak is still debated, Minister for Health Jeremiah Doughnut has instructed all infected adults and children to stay away from school and their places of work in order to prevent the disease from spreading.'

I hung my head, knowing how pointless that was going to be.

The man went on. 'As we know, one of the weirder elements of this strange new disease is that every single head seems to be growing something different, which has made it hard to know what to call the outbreak, but one name seems to have stuck: Scalp Sprout.'

The camera cut away to the placards that were now bobbing up and down in the crowd, on which were written the words:

Save our town!

Stop the rot – stop the Scalp Sprout.

Heads are for hair! Keep Sterilis normal.

The man smirked. 'We'll be bringing you live updates on-site as and when they come through. One thing is for sure, however: this is a story that looks set to grow and grow. I'm Nathan Bites, and this is the news at two.'

Mum pressed a button on the remote and he disappeared.

I was so upset, I reached for my third brownie.

*

Half an hour later, there was a knock on the door.

I ran to open it and stood there for a moment, too surprised to say anything. Because it wasn't just Neena standing there with her mum and dad. Behind her stood Bertie, Elka and Robbie, as well as their parents.

Robbie's dad had a head that was covered in long

golden straw like a mane of blond hair. Here and there I saw tiny mice peeping out shyly.

'Can we come in?' he asked nervously. 'Before anyone else sees us?'

'Hello, love,' said Mrs Gupta, giving me a more normal smile from under a head covered in pink roses. 'Heard you and your mum had both sprouted. Thought we'd better check in on you both.'

'They bumped into us on the way,' explained Elka, 'and we thought we'd come along too.'

Behind Elka was her mum, with tall reddish-pink stalks sticking out of her head. 'Rhubarb,' she said glumly.

'We were going stir-crazy at home,' added Robbie, pulling at his pink flowers anxiously.

'If we're going to suffer, we might as well suffer together,' added Bertie, staring at the ground.

There was a bustling sound behind me, and Mum appeared. 'Come in,' she said, smiling widely. 'I'll put the kettle on.'

A few moments later, Cheery Cottage was full of people for the first time since my ill-fated fifth birthday party. They sat on the sofa, the armchair, the coffee table, the window ledge and finally the floor.

As word spread that there was a support group for Scalp Sprout sufferers at our home, more people arrived: neighbours, kids from our school, their parents and siblings. As they squeezed into our tiny lounge, the air became rich with the smells from their heads: honey tangs, hints of smoky sweetness, the musk of hay and roses.

Once everybody had gathered, we all fell silent in the lounge. We looked nervously at each other, not quite knowing what to say.

Finally, Robbie's dad brushed the golden mane away from his face and spoke abruptly. 'This is a disaster,' he said.

'A catastrophe,' agreed Neena's mother.

'A curse,' said Elka's mother.

'A nightmare,' said someone else.

Then everybody started shouting at once.

'It's in the air!'

'It's in our blood!'

'It's the water!'

'It's a joke!'

'I feel like I'm in a dream!'

'In a nightmare, more like!'

'We need doctors!'

'We need help!'

'Operations!'

'Government aid!'

'Let's start with tea,' said Mum gently. 'What will everyone have?'

*

Over the next half hour, we made six pots of tea with extra sugar ('For the shock,' said Mum) and gave out brownies, cheese sandwiches and a batch of flapjacks that Mum somehow managed to knock up in about five minutes.

While Neena and I stayed in the kitchen, buttering bread and slicing cheese, I heard sighs of appreciation float down the hallway as Mum took plates of food into the lounge. Once we'd finished our jobs, we followed her, keen to get our fill.

The atmosphere felt completely different in the room – that panicky feeling had gone, and the parents looked less worried as they wiped chocolate crumbs from their lips and refilled their mugs. Robbie was even doing his best impression of Mr Grittysnit, stalking about and staring at everybody's head with bulging eyes, while the parents tried hard not to laugh. It almost felt like a party – as close to a party as you could get in the middle of a traumatising epidemic, obviously. And in the middle of it all sat Mum, chatting away to the people around her, her cheeks glowing for the first time in ages.

Once everyone had eaten, reassured each other and promised ongoing moral support, my sleepy classmates were bundled away by their parents.

Neena's mum stood on the doorstep with a funny look in her eyes. 'I'd forgotten how good your brownies are,' she said, hugging Mum goodbye.

'Do you remember our plans when the girls were babies?' Mum said.

'The café,' said Mrs Gupta, her face lighting up in a way that suddenly made her look younger. 'Why didn't we do it, Trix?'

'Oh, you know. We got those temping jobs to earn a bit of money to get it off the ground, and then . . . life got in the way.'

I stared at the two women, wondering why they were both sighing and smiling in that sad sort of way again.

CHAPTER 40

ONCE MUM AND I had done the dishes and gone to bed, I'd had a strange, unsettled night, plagued by dreams in which little children with ant mounds on their faces pointed fingers at me and Neena, shouting, 'You did this! You!', and an old woman fluttered around me, her face blazing with revenge.

In the morning, I threw a hopeful look in the mirror, which didn't last long, obviously, because my growth was still there in all its rank grow-y glory. My grass looked a bit less green, though, than it had before. I looked closer. That wasn't the only thing that looked like it was suffering; my flowers were too. Possibly because they needed water, or sunlight, or something.

I stared at them malevolently. *Well, they can think on. I'm not going to look after them. The less attention they get, the quicker they can die and my life can get back to normal.*

I walked into the kitchen to find Mum huddled

over the tiny radio on the kitchen counter, wearing her grubby yellow dressing gown. I noticed that the tiny leaves on her head tree were curled up at the edges. She held her fingers up to her lips when she saw me and pointed at the radio.

'. . . with twenty new outbreaks of Scalp Sprout reported this morning alone, it appears that this terrifying new epidemic shows no sign of abating,' said a serious male voice. 'So, stay safe, local residents. The medical advice for this outbreak is to remain at home, in order to stop this disease from spreading. Also, do not attempt to pull out any growths yourself – we've heard from several parents that this has led to extreme agony, and in some cases only serves to make the growth more rigorous, which none of us wants . . .'

I glanced outside at the backyard. There was the hideous old willow tree, its roots smothered underneath Vinnie's fresh layer of concrete. Its branches waved at me in the breeze, as if taunting me again. I turned away from the window pointedly.

'Well, if we're not allowed out of the house, I'm going to spend the morning applying for jobs,' Mum said, cracking an egg. 'What do you fancy doing?'

I shrugged, and glanced at my schedule. 'Well,

today's a Wednesday, which means I normally give my room a clean after After-school Club. I could do that now. I guess.'

As I dragged my feet up the stairs, my eyes fell on the group of framed photographs on the wall.

One showed me in the Little Sterilis Soft Play Centre when I was about two. I was holding a white plastic telephone and staring at it in a confused sort of way. Harsh electric lights lit my face. Behind me, as a blurry background, I could just make out the nets that surrounded the ball pit. It looked like I'd been thrown into a netted toddler prison.

At that age, I thought suddenly, Agatha Strangeways was probably playing with the wild flowers and butterflies in the meadows around her – our – house.

I was surprised to find myself wondering what she would have made of the windowless, underground play centre where I'd spent so much of my childhood.

But where else could Mum have taken me? The shopping centre? The bingo hall? The tanning salon? It wasn't her fault that there was nowhere else to take me.

Not by then.

I went to my room slowly.

I was just in the middle of sorting my school shirts when my mobile rang.

Neena sounded cheerful. 'Are you enjoying your morning off?'

'Not really.' My hand went up to my temples automatically, as if to rub my worries away, when I remembered what I would touch. I yanked my hand back down, just in time. 'What are you up to?'

'I'm writing up the entire "Suprising Seeds" experiement, actually. There's so much to put in—'

'You can't do that! This is a *secret*, Neena. We agreed we wouldn't tell *anyone*. You can't go writing about it—'

'Oh, don't worry, I won't show it to anyone. But I'm a scientist. This is what scientists do – they record their results. I'm watching the news too, just to make the report as up to date as possible, of course. Did you know that there's a group of local parents who are going to be marching around outside the school gates in half an hour in protest?'

'What for?'

'They're protesting for their children's right to have a normal education, no matter what their heads look like. It's all going to kick off. You should check out the news – at least it's a chance to watch Mr Grittysnit trying to deal with a mob of angry parents, which should be fun.'

A reluctant grin spread across my face. 'I might.'

'You know, you could just put everyone out of their misery and tell the truth.' Neena's voice was gentle but persistent.

'No! It's got to be kept a secret – there's t-too much to lose—' I stammered.

Down the phone, her voice was firm. 'If you tell the truth now, at least all those people would get the answers they're demanding. We could explain together. We could say that it wasn't your fault—'

'Oh yeah! And *what* would we explain? That I heard a dead woman's voice in my brain, telling me to sprinkle some random seeds on our heads, and I just went ahead and did it? Do you think they'd believe any of it? Why don't you just walk me to the bus stop in the morning and wave me on to the Western Poorcrumble school bus while you're at it, because if anyone finds out, that's where I'm going.'

I found it hard to keep my voice quiet, as my anger began to thrash around inside me.

'Okay, okay,' Neena sighed. 'Point taken. Talk later?'

'Okay. Bye.' I hung up.

Distracted and unhappy, I stood at my bedroom window and gazed out on to our road. After a moment or two, a group of grey-haired women in fleeces appeared. All of them were wearing transparent shower caps on their heads, a little like the protective hats Mum had to wear in the factory.

One of them stopped and looked at a map. 'I think the school is this way,' she said in a loud clear voice, pointing in the direction of Grittysnits.

The others squealed and clapped their hands.

'How exciting!' said one. 'I can't wait to see them close up.'

'Me neither,' said another, digging a camera out from her rucksack. 'This was worth the three-hour trip on the motorway, wasn't it, girls?'

'Just don't forget – *no touching them,*' said another as she pulled a little plastic bottle out of her handbag and squirted its contents on to her hands, before passing the bottle around the group.

'I wonder if that dreamboat Nathan Bites will be at the school again,' said one, rearranging her hair-cap carefully. 'Such a great idea, Patricia. I mean, we've been to Stonehenge so many times, but this . . . Well, this is a great suggestion. Really *thrilling*.'

'Come on, quick – if we hurry to the school gates we might see some fresh sprouters,' barked a lady in a waxed green jacket.

They trotted off down the road in their sensible shoes.

From my window, I watched them depart, feeling confused. *Who are they? And what do they mean, better than Stonehenge and 'worth the three-hour trip'? Are they visiting Little Sterilis on purpose?*

The penny dropped.

They were tourists.

And they were just the first.

CHAPTER 41

I wandered downstairs and flicked the telly on.

Neena was right: the protest had started in earnest outside our school. Mr Grittysnit had resumed his position as the gatekeeper, scowling at the parents and placards crowding around him.

A woman in a rainbow-coloured woollen poncho held a loudspeaker up to her mouth. 'Quarantine is really cruel, let our children go to school,' she chanted, her other hand raised up in a fist.

'QUARANTINE IS REALLY CRUEL, LET OUR CHILDREN GO TO SCHOOL,' shouted the parents.

'Doesn't matter if they're grassy, let our children back to classy,' shouted the woman, her voice hoarse.

'DOESN'T MATTER IF THEY'RE GRASSY, LET OUR CHILDREN—'

'Listen! Listen!' barked Mr Grittysnit. Once the crowd was quiet, he spoke. 'Your children are infected.

There's a quarantine to observe. *I* didn't make the rules – it's medical advice.'

'Yeah, well, those doctors may not get paid by the hour, but I do, and every hour I'm at home with the twins cos of this quarantine, I'm losing money, and we need to eat,' said a burly bloke flanked by two boys with bright-red strawberry plants on their heads. He shoved the boys in front of him. 'Go on, you two. In you go. You look healthy enough to me,' he said.

His sons walked towards the gates, but Mr Grittysnit stood in front of them and crossed his arms. 'They're diseased. They're not allowed in. Rules are rules.'

Their father began to walk, slowly but with purpose, towards our headmaster.

The crowd went quiet. Several grown-ups took a step back as the muscly man stood in front of Mr Grittysnit, dwarfing him easily.

The boys with the strawberry plants looked uncertainly from their father to Mr Grittysnit, their pasty faces anxious.

Mr Grittysnit gulped, but he stood firm. 'I told you before. Unsprouted heads only—'

Suddenly he stopped talking. He clutched his head and gave an agonised shriek.

In our lounge, the TV screen suddenly filled with an unpleasant close-up of Mr Grittysnit's face, while the presenter said, 'Stand by for live and exclusive footage of a Scalp Sprout happening. Might the head of the Head be next?'

Dark brown ridges began to cover Mr Grittysnit's shiny bald scalp.

'He's got tree bark on his head,' gasped the news announcer.

Then Mr Grittysnit's hands flew up to his nose. He made a movement as if to turn away back towards the school, but the man in front of him quickly grabbed his hand and pulled it down from his nose.

The crowd shrieked. The camera wobbled. On the screen was a blurry image of something pink and wriggly sticking out of Mr Grittysnit's two large nostrils. He yanked his hand back to cover them, but the screen was then filled with a replay, in close-up, of the pale squirmy things we'd seen poking out of the dark holes.

They were *worms*. Mr Grittysnit glared at the crowd for a second and then scuttled away towards the school.

The burly man turned to the camera. 'Well,' he said, grinning, 'that's a sprouter if ever I saw one. Which means he ain't got no right to exclude anyone, as far as

I'm concerned. In you go, fellas. See you at home time.'

He gave the kids a gentle push and they walked into the schoolyard.

The crowd of parents gave a roar of approval and the woman in the rainbow poncho brought the megaphone back up towards her mouth. 'Now he's sprouted, we are sure, he can't keep them out no more . . .'

As the crowd picked up the chant, I pulled my droopy flowers and browning grass hair back into a tight ponytail and packed my school bag. Because, Scalp Sprout or not, I still had a competition to win.

CHAPTER 42

By MIDDAY, EVERY single Grittysnit child was back at school and, on the face of it, things were carrying on as normal, give or take the odd pained shriek echoing down the corridor from another fresh Scalp Sprout victim.

The corridors still smelled of cabbage. The Valentini construction crew were still hammering away at the new exam hall. We were all still safely inside our classrooms, while the sunshine beamed on to the empty concrete yard outside.

Chrissie Valentini was still being unbearable. She kept touching her perfect red French braid deliberately, as if to draw attention to the fact that she hadn't sprouted anything. 'Mummy and Daddy *begged* me to stay at home so I wouldn't catch the bug,' I heard her drawling to Bella behind me. 'But I thought *someone* at this school has to set a good example.'

'And what an example,' said Bella. 'I feel *blessed*.'

'You are. Plus, I have an incredible immune system and a private doctor, so I'm not at risk. But, honestly, you would not believe how much Mummy and Daddy pleaded with me to stay. They said all the shopping and business lunches and spa visits they get up to when I'm at school don't make up for the loneliness of the mansion when I'm not there. They looked totally gutted as Blenkinsop drove me to school.'

'Well, they would be,' said Bella.

So, yeah, not much change there, then.

But *something* had changed.

My school – my second home, practically – felt suddenly alien to me. It felt wrong. It felt airless. It felt stuffy. It felt miserable. It felt . . . impossible to concentrate. It made my skin itch. With all the windows shut, and a large heavy roof over my head, I felt smothered and trapped in the classroom. My face kept rotating towards the light. My heart yearned for something I couldn't describe. And my ponytail of floppy flowers looked worse every time I looked in the mirror. My mossy forehead was as dry and scratchy as an old pot scourer.

I wasn't the only one finding it hard to concentrate, either.

My classmates gazed listlessly out of the window and up at the clouds rolling slowly by, sighing and huffing and puffing, and all their heads were in a similar sorry state too.

Neena, who had dragged her feet all the way to school, seemed to have given up all pretence of caring about schoolwork, and had begun to scribble away feverishly in her yellow notebook almost as soon as we'd sat down.

And I wasn't the only one to notice.

'You're a busy bee, aren't you?' Chrissie jeered.

Neena whipped round and glared at her. 'So what if I am?' she snapped.

'What are you writing anyway?' asked Chrissie. 'Doesn't look like Spanish verbs.'

Neena covered her book up quickly, but not before an awful thought crossed my mind. She hadn't been so recklessly stupid as to bring her notebook into school, had she? The one which went into, with horrible accuracy, our experiment with the Surprising Seeds and which could drop us into a whole load of trouble if anyone found it . . . Had she?

Chrissie raised her hand, her face lit up with triumph. 'Er, Miss Mossheart? I would like to report . . .'

But then her voice trailed off.

She gasped. She shrieked. She clutched her head.

As we watched, a tiny tip of a purple stem began to poke out of the glossy French plait on Chrissie's scalp. Then it grew taller and wider.

Everybody in the class had turned round in their desks to stare, exchanging fascinated whispers about what Chrissie would grow.

But after a few seconds, as the purple horn thing growing out of her head got bigger, the excited whispers turned to horrified gagging noises. Everybody began to flinch. Kids held their noses. As the stench rolled its way through the classroom, there were gasps of horror and cries of 'Pooh whiff!'

At the top of the purple stem danced a green flower that ended in dark frilly pleats. From the middle of the flower emerged a long purple tube, which looked like a pointing finger. And it was easily the stinkiest, smelliest, pongiest case of Scalp Sprout that we had seen. Next to it, Bella's mushroom seemed as fragrant as a posh air freshener. It made me yearn for a whiff of the school lavatories instead, which would have been like a breath of fresh air in comparison.

Because the thick green flower, sticking out of

Chrissie's scalp like a hand sticking out of a grave, had a smell disgusting enough to strip the skin from your nostrils.

Oh, the smell! It made Elka faint. It made Bertie run to the wastepaper basket and be sick into it.

'Get me out of here,' moaned Aisha, running for the door.

'Someone open the window!' cried Robbie, scrabbling at the locks with his eyes streaming.

The smell got stronger and more disgusting with every second.

Chrissie stared at us, confused. 'Is it a rose?' she asked uncertainly, touching the atrocity on her scalp with hesitant hands.

'Nog esacdly,' said Bella, who was holding her nose firmly.

'It's a corpse flower,' said Miss Mossheart. 'One of the rarest in the world.'

Chrissie preened. 'Well, that makes sense,' she bragged.

'It's called a corpse flower,' gagged Miss Mossheart, taking several steps back as the smell intensified, 'because, when it blooms, it smells of badly rotting meat. And, Chrissie –' our teacher adopted the extremely solemn face of somebody trying hard not to laugh – 'I'm afraid they have a lifespan of about forty years.'

Chrissie turned towards Bella, shouting, 'Cut it off. Now!'

Bella backed away from her desk. 'Jud remembered, er, a prior apoingment.' And she ran towards the door on surprisingly speedy skinny legs.

'Where are you going?' asked Chrissie, her green eyes narrowed.

'Eggywhere else,' replied Bella, gasping. 'Eggywhere will goo. Bye!'

We all ran outside the classroom, leaving Chrissie sitting at her desk, looking unsure of herself and holding her nose. We crowded round the classroom door, looking in through the window, as if Chrissie was an unusual specimen in the zoo.

Miss Mossheart took a few deep inhalations of air. 'Maybe if we keep all the windows open she can still take part in the lesson.'

'As long as we dangle her outside,' muttered Robbie.

I laughed despite myself, and Chrissie must have heard me, because her head snapped up and she glared at me. Then she grinned horribly and, leaning over, picked up the notebook on Neena's desk, which I now saw that Neena must have abandoned in her desperate scrabble to get away from the smell.

No!

'What's she reading?' asked Bertie. 'It must be really bad. Look how cross she is.'

My hands darted out for the door handle. 'Let me back in,' I pleaded.

Twenty pairs of hands drew me back.

'No way,' said Robbie. 'If you open that door, we'll all die from the fumes.'

Helpless, I could only stand there and watch Chrissie as she flicked through the pages of Neena's notebook, her eyes widening at every word.

'Just *how* thorough were your notes?' I whispered to Neena.

She looked proud of herself and also a little sheepish. 'It was the most complete write-up I have ever done. I left no detail out. Sorry.'

I lunged at the door again.

Elka beat me to it and stared at me. 'Have you got some sort of death wish?' she asked.

I gave up.

Ever so slowly, Chrissie put the notebook down and

stared at me through the glass. She gave me a strange, slightly haunted look, and I wondered if she'd got to the bit where her family had poisoned and cheated and lied to get their hands on the Cherrybliss land. Then again, I thought, watching the smirk now spreading across her face, perhaps she hadn't.

Chrissie pushed her chair away and walked towards the door.

Everybody shrank away and pressed themselves against the wall.

'Steel your nostrils!' shouted Robbie.

I threw an agonised look at Neena.

The door opened and Chrissie walked out with her head held high and Neena's incriminating notebook in her hands.

Everybody moaned as she walked past us and headed straight to Mr Grittysnit's office.

I moaned loudest of all when I realised what she was up to.

There was just enough time to catch the sound of Mr Grittysnit retching before Chrissie shut his office door, her face lit up with a dark victory.

CHAPTER 43

At least Mr Grittysnit and Chrissie looked like they were enjoying our expulsion, even if I wasn't.

'Effective immediately,' said Mr Grittysnit.

At least, I think that's what he said. He was pinching his nose the whole time; Chrissie's smell was maturing by the second.

I looked down at his grey carpet, squirming with fury. This wouldn't be happening if Neena hadn't been so *stupid*. I sneaked a look at her in frustration. Oblivious, she was staring at Mr Grittysnit as if she'd like to stick him into a large jar of formaldehyde. In the meantime, he was glaring at me. Talk about a hate triangle.

'Well, I'm glad,' Neena blurted out defiantly. 'I was getting really tired of being at a school that kept telling me how bad I am at following the rules and ignoring all the things I'm actually good at. I'm not bad, and neither is Sorrel.'

'How sweet, sticking up for your friend,' he replied

smoothly. 'When she was in here, only yesterday, betraying you for an Obedience Point.'

Neena gasped, and I stared at the carpet again.

As the frosty silence grew between us, Chrissie smirked. 'Well, I guess this is goodbye. Enjoy your time at Poorcrumble. Does this mean I can have another Obedience Point, sir?'

Underneath Chrissie's jeering words, I thought I heard a trace of something else in her voice. I'd spent so much time wanting to win the competition I'd never thought to wonder why she wanted to. I mean, it wasn't as if she *needed* a week in Portugal – not with all those holiday homes we heard so much about.

The way she'd asked for those Obedience Points had sounded almost . . . desperate. Was she trying to win someone's approval too? And why had she banged on so much about the way her parents had begged her to stay at home that morning?

A twinge of pity ran through me. It *was* kind of weird how Chrissie went to Breakfast Club *and* After-school Club every single day, even though her mum didn't work. How she often talked about going to the shops and the cinema with her chauffeur or one of their maids. And when that throng of parents had stormed the gates demanding for the kids to be let loose, I remembered Chrissie standing all alone in the school grounds, glancing at the watch on her wrist.

Maybe she hadn't been admiring the precision of its Swiss engineering. Maybe she'd been wondering when someone would show up for her.

'Why are you still here?' demanded Mr Grittysnit, interrupting my thoughts.

We left his office and, seconds later, Neena's notebook landed with a slam beside us on the carpet.

Neena bent down to pick it up. She heaved a huge sigh of relief as she flicked through it. 'Phew,' she said. 'No pages ripped. That would have been awful.'

'Oh, *that* would have been awful?' I asked through gritted teeth. 'We've just been expelled, it's the worst day of my life, I have daisy stalks for eyebrows, but at least your stupid notebook is okay?'

She stood up and jutted her chin out. 'Don't talk to *me* like that, Sorrel. Why did you tell on me yesterday? We're meant to be *best friends*, or have you forgotten? Were you so desperate for Grittysnit's approval that you lost your marbles as well as your hair?'

The river of anger running through me seemed dangerously close to breaking its banks. 'At least I cared about doing well. All you've ever cared about is your crusty science rubbish. Didn't it cross your mind that if you brought your stupid notebook to school, our secret would be found out? Didn't you even think?' I snapped.

Neena twitched her head. 'Don't call it stupid,' she said in a warning tone.

I narrowed my eyes. A need to lash out grew in me. 'It *is* a stupid notebook. And you got me expelled.'

She flushed red. '*You* got yourself expelled. *You* found the Surprising Seeds. *You* were the one batty enough to hear voices. It was *your* idea to put them on our heads! So don't you dare try to blame this all on me!'

The corridor filled with the sound of our rapid breathing. My jaw muscles tensed, like a cobra desperate to strike one final time.

'Yeah, you're right,' I said slowly, exasperation twisting my mouth into grotesque shapes. '*I* found the packet. *I* heard the voice. *I* sprinkled the Seeds. In fact, when I really think about it, you did absolutely nothing apart from tag along after me like some irritating shadow. Put *that* in your stupid notebook.'

As soon as the words were out of my mouth, I wanted to claw them back.

'I'm sorry, Neena. I really am. I didn't mean it.'

Her brown eyes narrowed and then looked away. 'If you think what I care about is so stupid, I'm not going to take up any more of your precious time.'

She took a deep breath, and something in her face was like a door slamming. 'And the next time you turn around and need me, I won't be there.' She shot me a bitter grin. 'And then you'll know *exactly* how it feels to be friends with you.'

She spun away from me and walked towards the double doors.

By the time I'd caught my breath and run out on to the tarmac to find her, she was nowhere to be seen.

CHAPTER 44

AND, BECAUSE I clearly hadn't suffered enough, I still had to face Mum back at home.

I'd just put my key in the front door when it opened slowly.

Her mobile phone was clutched in her hand. 'I've been having an interesting chat with Mr Grittysnit,' she said in a flat voice. 'You'd better come in.'

I walked inside, heart thudding, and followed Mum as she padded silently into the kitchen. The table was covered with the job-vacancies page of the local newspaper.

She pushed them to the side roughly and pointed to the chair. 'Sit.'

I sat.

'Is it true,' she said, 'that all of this . . . Scalp Sprout . . . is because of *you*? Some prank you cooked up with Neena? You were behind it all along, and you pretended you had no idea how it happened?'

Every time I'd imagined Mum finding out, I'd

thought she'd get angry and shout. Nothing had prepared me for the sadness.

'Mum—' I tried, but she held a shaking hand up.

'Sorrel, do you realise what you've done?'

I hung my head. 'I've turned everybody into freaks?' I volunteered.

'Worse than that. You lied to them. You never came forward and told the truth. Perhaps if you had, the doctors would have found it easier to cure Scalp Sprout. Do you *know* how busy the local hospitals are? And you never told *me* the truth. I had to find out about it from that ogre of a man. I thought you were better than that.'

'I'm sorry,' I mumbled, but she seemed not to hear me.

'And the worst thing, Sorrel, is that you've brought an entire media circus to this town, who, at this very minute, are pointing their cameras at little boys and little girls and making them embarrassed about who they are. *That* is worse than anything.' Mum's disappointment in me seemed to fill the entire kitchen. It silenced even the tap.

'On a more practical level, Sorrel, your pranks have caused me to lose my job.' She looked at the circled vacancies by her side and sighed. 'It's funny how I don't have many career options after being fired from one of the only employers in town.'

I gazed at her defeated eyes and tried to explain. 'The thing is, Mum, I did this for us.'

She shot me an angry look. 'Don't tease me, Sorrel – I'm not in the mood.'

'But I did!' Tears spilled down my face. 'I found the Seeds . . . There was a voice . . . which said I'd change your life . . . our life . . . And you looked as if you needed the holiday so badly, Mum . . .'

She frowned. 'What holiday?'

I stared at her. *Is she joking?* 'The holiday in Portugal! The prize for the most obedient pupil. I thought the Seeds would help me win, and then you'd be happy, and . . .'

Mum was shaking her head. 'I never asked you to win that holiday, sweetheart. *I* didn't care about the holiday – you did! I just went along with it because I wanted you to be happy.'

'What? You went along with it for me? But I was doing it for you! I did it to cheer you up.'

'Cheer me up?' Mum stared at me across the table, and she gave a funny half sob, half laugh. 'You thought that it was *your* job to cheer *me* up?'

She took a deep breath, and muttered to herself, 'Oh, I've properly stuffed things up here, haven't I?'

I stared at her, confused, and she gave me a shaky smile. 'Listen, Sorrel, I know I can be a bit gloomy at times, but that should never have been your problem. If you really want to know the truth, I hated working in a freezing factory all day long, watching huge tubes of processed meat pour out of a machine. I never wanted that for myself. I was sick and tired of not having the guts to stand up to my boss, and always being too exhausted to have fun with you, and . . . not being the mum you deserved. *That* was why I was gloomy.'

'You never liked working at Chillz? But I thought you loved it!'

She grimaced. 'I know you did, and it was easier for me that way. If you'd known the truth, you would have worried about me. And I guess I –' her lips wobbled – 'wanted to protect you from the mess I'd made of my life.' She looked down at the table, and roughly brushed her eyes.

We were quiet for what felt like a hundred years. The clock in the hallway ticked over us.

'Looks like we were both keeping secrets from each other then,' I said finally.

She gave me a tired grin, her green eyes brimming with unshed tears. 'Looks like it.'

An unsettling thought crossed my mind. 'So, all those Perfect Behaviour certificates, all the Full Attendance records I got at school, all those shoeboxes of awards . . . were they just a waste of time?'

Mum hesitated, then gave a tiny shrug. 'To be honest, I wouldn't have cared if you'd come back with certificates for the Fluffiest Tummy Button, as long as you were doing what you loved and working out what you were put on this earth to do. That's what I wanted for you more than anything, so you wouldn't end up in a pair of overalls you never wanted to wear. I've been proud of you since the day you were born. I didn't need any certificates from that school to prove to me how amazing you are.'

'But you called me your good girl and you looked so much happier when I came home with awards.'

Mum sighed. 'I was happy because it seemed to matter so much to you. I thought all that stuff was what you wanted, and I said well done because it looked important to you.'

She fiddled with the silver hoops in her ears and sighed. 'This is my fault. I should have said this to you much, much earlier, then maybe we wouldn't be in this mess.' She glanced up at me and a smile darted about her lips. 'But the good news is, I've had a brilliant idea, Sorrel. Ever since Neena's mum reminded me about that café we were going to—'

The knock on the door was firm but loud.

Mum frowned. 'Are you expecting anyone?'

I shook my head.

'Well, is there any chance you might be able to get the door? Whoever it is, say we're busy. We've got so much to talk about—'

Bang, bang, bang.

'Crumbs, someone's insistent,' said Mum.

'Back in a sec,' I said, pushing my chair back.

I walked down the corridor, my heart all mixed up. There was sadness in there, yes, but also hope. It had been good to be honest with Mum. I felt like there was a tiny glimmer of light in front of me.

I opened the front door and was blinded by a popping flashbulb.

'Well now, isn't that a happy smile for a girl who's in so much trouble?' said an oily voice.

Once my eyes had adjusted, I peered at the man in a tight pink suit standing in front of me. Something about his eyes looked familiar.

'W-what?' I stammered.

He smoothed back his slick blond hair and bared his teeth. 'Don't you mean "pardon"?' he said silkily.

I frowned as my mind whirred with questions. Why did I recognise him? Who was the woman standing behind him on our gravel path? Why was she holding a huge camera and giving me a strangely intense smile? Why did I feel like a frog about to be dissected in a biology lesson? And *what* was that horrible smell? And—

'Sorry Fallowfield?' asked the man pleasantly, whipping out a notebook from his pocket and a pencil with a sharp black point.

'Yes?' I said, too surprised to correct him on my actual name.

'I'm Nathan Bites, head reporter from *National Scoops*,' he said. 'I've been told you might know something about the Scalp Sprout epidemic. Do you want to tell your side of the story?'

'Say that again?' I asked, stalling for time.

Nathan's eyes narrowed. 'Come on, fess up, girl. I've got an extremely reliable source who's told us practically *everything*. The guilt must be crushing you.

Why not tell me *all* about it?'

'Who are you?' said Mum behind me. 'What are you doing doorstepping my daughter?'

Nathan and the camerawoman looked as thrilled as if we'd just passed them plates of their favourite pudding.

'Oh, it's the touching duo,' Nathan crooned. 'How nice to see you again. What's it like, Mum, to know your daughter is the mastermind of this horrific plague? To know that she's behind that ridiculous tree on your head? Don't let me put words into your mouth, obviously, but shall we start with ashamed? Disgusted?'

'How about *clear off*?' said Mum as she touched her growth self-consciously.

'I don't think that was one of the options on offer, Mum,' I murmured.

Nathan tilted his head at her, as if she'd disappointed him. Then he shrugged and pointed his pencil at me. 'Fine, back to the daughter, then. Tell me why you did it, Sorry. Are you harbouring a grudge against your classmates? Did you need a bit of attention – was that it? I hear your dad left when you were young – that must have messed you up—'

'That's enough!' exploded Mum, the leaves on her

tree rustling angrily. 'Are you mad? Stop making this stuff up. She's only eleven! She's not a mastermind – she's just an ordinary girl who made a silly mistake. This was an *accident*, and actually she did it all because she wanted to make me proud of her—'

Nathan's eyes lit up. '*Really?* So your daughter carried out this awful plot to please you? Wow, this story just gets better and better.'

'So many angles,' said the woman behind him, nodding fervently.

'Oh, don't be stupid,' snapped Mum. 'Wherever do you get these ideas from? Anyway, how did you find out our address?'

Nathan said smoothly, 'I don't reveal my sources.'

But he didn't have to. I could smell his source. And it was standing on the pavement right outside our house, waving gleefully.

'Hi, Chrissie,' I said flatly.

Mum's eyes watered as her nose encountered the corpse flower. 'What's that disgusting smell?'

I sighed. 'It's Chrissie, Mum.'

'I thought some drains had burst—'

Nathan butted in, 'Come on, Sorry, tell us how you did it and we'll leave you alone. Put the record straight.

Better out than in. You'll feel better for it, once this is all out in the open – I say that to everyone, because it's true.' His voice was as low and insistent as a fly buzzing around my head.

The blood began to pound in my temples.

'Go on, Sorry, you know you want to,' he pestered. 'What's the matter, cat got your tongue? Give us the exclusive and I'll make you the most famous eleven-year-old in the country. You'll be in all the papers. Wouldn't you like that?'

I stared at his jutting face and his ravenous eyes. Why couldn't he get my name right?

Something inside me snapped.

'I'M NOT SORRY!' I screamed.

Flash! The camera clicked.

'Got it,' said the woman. 'That was a good one. Really captured her evil side. I can see this going viral.'

'IT'S SORREL,' I shouted. 'Like the herb?'

'Whatever,' said the woman, turning to go.

Nathan, meanwhile, was halfway towards the National Scoops van. 'Hostile single mother, brainwashed latchkey kid, unwarranted threats and a neglected home – is it any wonder that Sorry turned out the way she did?' he said aloud, as if he was rehearsing a speech, giving us one final, lingering look as he folded himself into the front seat.

'Oh, take a swim in a vat of hair gel,' Mum barked.

Just before she slammed the front door shut, I saw the wide satisfied grins on the faces of Chrissie, Nathan and the camerawoman. They'd obviously got what they wanted – but what was that, exactly?

CHAPTER 45

WHATEVER ELSE YOU could say about Nathan Bites – and Mum had plenty – he was as good as his word. He did make me famous.

The very next morning, I was plastered all over the national papers. From the *Sterilis Standard* to the *Daily Splash*, those pictures of me and Mum squinting into the camera were on every front page in the country, as well as some rather nasty headlines, like: *'I'm not sorry!' Mastermind of Terrifying Epidemic Remains Unrepentant* and *Does This Freakish Plague Mean the End of the World? When Will It Stop? How Will It End?* and *The Seedy Secret Home Life of Britain's Naughtiest Eleven-year-old* and *How to Protect Yourself from an Outbreak: Harness the Power of My Tailor-made Crystals by Dr Phoney Maloney*. The pictures of my scowling face, dried-up forehead and floppy flowers didn't paint me in the best possible light, I had to admit.

Over the course of the morning, the telly and

the radio and the internet began to repeat the same rubbish that Nathan had dreamed up. How I'd concocted a hideous experiment with my best friend Neena in her shed. How we'd created the Surprising Seeds using a mixture of dangerous chemicals and witchcraft. Whatever Chrissie had told Nathan clearly hadn't involved the truth about Agatha Strangeways and where the Surprising Seeds really had come from. Either she'd been too ashamed of what she'd read about her ancestors, hadn't been able to read Neena's terrible handwriting or she didn't get to that part in the notebook. Either way, without that crucial part of the story going public, I had to admit that we did look pretty evil.

Should I set the record straight? But who on earth would believe me?

Meanwhile, Mum spent the morning running around our house turning off the telly and the radio and putting her mobile on silent, saying she couldn't bear it any more, and then just a few minutes later she'd turn them back on again, saying it was better to know the worst. She looked so overwhelmed and frightened I felt that any more revelations would tip her over the edge.

The crowd of journalists and tourists moved from

their patch by the school gates to right outside our house. Their excited yakking as they huddled on the pavement could be heard even from our kitchen. Mum had to keep the curtains in the lounge shut because people kept sticking their mobiles up to the windows to try to get a picture of us.

And every few seconds it felt as if somebody was knocking on our door, hoping for us to say something else that would make everybody in the country hate us all over again. The journalists even shouted questions through the letter box.

'Is there anything else you want to share?'

'Are you cooking up any more of those Surprising Seeds in there?'

'What's your next trick?'

'Any chance I can use your bathroom?'

Mum stifled a scream and turned the volume on the radio up louder, and our kitchen was filled with the voice of a news reporter announcing: 'And finally, news just in. The entire town of Little Sterilis has been infected by Scalp Sprout.'

Mum and I stared at each other.

It's exactly what Agatha Strangeways wanted.

'Doctors are still no closer to finding a cure for the

thousands infected, although they can confirm that, so far, only the residents of this town have been afflicted by the disease. We understand that this is all the work of one eleven-year-old girl, Sorry Fallowfield, the product of a broken home –' Mum gasped – 'and her gormless partner-in-crime, Neena Gupta, who we believe is no longer speaking to her.'

I sniffed. *Go on, rub it in.*

The reporter's voice became more animated. 'Speaking to us by a live link this morning are some of their victims, their very own classmates from Grittysnits School. Robbie, Bella, Bertie and Elka . . . hello.'

'Hello,' they said, sounding uncertain.

My mouth went dry as I heard the muted sounds of my friends – and Bella.

'Tell us how you feel about this betrayal by your friends.'

'Well, we're upset – of course we are,' said Elka. 'But we're not sure they did all of this *deliberately.*'

'Y-yeah,' stammered a quiet voice that could only have been Bertie. 'It might have just been a mistake. They're our friends—'

'But they've deformed your heads,' the woman butted in. 'Don't you feel angry? Victimised? Betrayed?'

'Oh yeah, I feel all of those things,' replied an eager voice. Bella. 'Definitely. Hungry, villainised, beshaved . . .'

I'd heard enough.

'I can't listen to this any more,' I said, feeling distraught. 'I'm going to my room.'

Mum opened her arms. 'Come here, love,' she said, but I shrugged her off and ran upstairs.

From my bedroom window, I could count at least fifty news vans crammed into our road. A little kiosk on wheels was in the middle of the pavement, and the teenager in the black hoodie was walking away from it, his arms full of takeaway coffee cups.

In front of our house, a woman with a huge mop of pink hair was wearing a T-shirt that read *Scalp Sprout Tours*. She was pointing at our home excitedly while a group of tourists clutching their mobile phones hung on to her every word.

And Nathan Bites, in prime position on our gravel path, seemed to be at the centre of it all. The make-up brush Kiki was dabbing on to his face was new and looked even bigger than his last one. 'How do I look?' he smirked at her, and the group of little old ladies nearby giggled and shrieked.

I checked my ancient mobile. Neena hadn't replied to *any* of the forty-five texts I'd sent her since our argument. I tried another. **Are *you* there? Are *you* okay? Please text me back. S x**

Despite all the horrible things being said about me on the radio and television, Neena's silence was by far the worst. And it went on all day.

CHAPTER 46

I CHECKED MY head in the mirror.

Yep. All still there. And it looked worse than ever.

But I was desperate to get out.

The press had been camped outside our house for three days. All Mum did now was sit on the sofa all day long, watching the news in her oldest and dirtiest pyjamas. The tree sticking out of her head had shed most of its leaves and the few that were left hung forlornly, like forgotten baubles on a Christmas tree. We'd run out of milk, teabags, bread and butter, and my brain felt dull and sluggish.

I smashed open my money box and pocketed my savings of £5.87.

'Mum,' I said firmly as I walked down the stairs, 'I'm going to the shop. Do you want anything?'

There was no reply. Mum was asleep on the sofa.

Did she not go to bed at all?

I looked a bit closer. The pallor of her skin could be seen through the gloom of the lounge.

I pushed open the front door.

The crowd outside gasped and backed away with hands over their heads, as if to protect themselves.

'Where are you going, duckie? Off to ruin everyone's lives? Oh no, my mistake – you've done that already.' Nathan smirked, as he poured half a bottle of Baby-blue Drops into his eyes.

I skulked past Nathan with my head down, while the flashbulbs and mobiles went ballistic around me.

I walked to the shop at the end of our road and ignored the pointed looks from the other customers inside. Once I'd picked up the essentials, I put my shopping on the counter and smiled at the woman behind it.

'Your money's no good here,' she said, scowling.

'Excuse me?' I said. I looked at the coins I'd put on the counter. They looked all right to me.

'I'm not serving you,' she spat. 'I know who you are. You ruined my ombré hairdo. It cost me two hundred quid, that did, and now all I have is this stupid red ivy creeper on the top of my head, and I hate it. So, I'm definitely not serving you.'

'But I'm so hungry. Please!' I begged.

She sniffed. 'Not my problem. Now clear off or I'll call security.'

I walked home, trying my hardest not to cry in the street.

And then I saw that someone had painted the words MASTERMIND SCALP SPROUT SCUM in bright red paint on our front door.

I gasped, excused my way through the crowd, which had got even bigger since I left the house, and pushed the door open, trying not to get red paint on my hands.

Once inside, I gave a despairing sniff. The house smelled musty and unwashed. Although Mum had woken up, she hadn't moved from the sofa, and something about the way she looked reminded me of the fly in Miss Mossheart's flytrap.

If she doesn't get up soon, I thought gloomily, *she'll probably disappear into its cushions for ever.*

My stomach gave an insistent rumble. I had a brainwave. We still had loads of Rejects in the freezer!

I stuck one in the oven, faintly surprised that the

usual cheesy smell filling the kitchen no longer made my mouth water.

Once the pizza had cooked, I took it into the lounge.

Mum was staring at the wall, fiddling with the hoops in her ears.

'How's the job search going?' I asked.

'No one wants to employ me, love,' she said flatly.

I caught a glimpse of the headline in the newspaper on the floor. *'We're Pulping All the Pizzas Made under Miss Fallowfield's Supervision,' Says Horrified Chillz Boss. 'It's the Least We Can Do.'*

Mum saw me looking at it and gave a hollow smile. 'I'm Little Sterilis's Worst Mother, apparently.'

'You're not,' I said quickly, but she just shrugged. 'Mum,' I said hesitantly, 'someone's painted something on our house.'

'Have they, love? That's nice,' she said dully.

'It says we're scum.'

'Oh well,' said Mum.

'Can we wash it off? I'll do it.'

'We've run out of washing-up liquid.'

'I'm sorry, Mum,' I said, taking in her pale face, wilted daisies and withered leaves.

'I know you are, love,' she sighed. 'I know you are.'

I bit into my Reject and spat out a mouthful of processed cheese. Something must have gone wrong at the factory recently – it tasted disgusting.

CHAPTER 47

AFTER SITTING IN the lounge listening to the scrum of journalists get louder and louder, I wandered upstairs to my room and sent Neena another text.

Can we talk? S xx

An unfamiliar sizzling noise drifted up from the pavement. I peeked out between my curtains. There was a sausage stand right outside our house. A man in a Hawaiian shirt was serving hot dogs to everyone. The smell made my stomach rumble. Blinking away my tears, I turned away from the window.

But the crowd began to buzz excitedly, and a huddle formed at the end of the road. I peered out but couldn't see beyond the glare of the flashbulbs. It was probably just another food vendor, I thought glumly, turning away from the view. If they were that excited, it would be doughnuts, or something.

Woof! Woof! A ferocious bark ripped through the air.

The crowd shrank away slightly, revealing Sid, a clump of bright yellow flowers sticking out of his head, and Florence by his side. Together they were slowly making their way up our road. I felt a mixture of happiness and fury when I saw him. What were *they* doing here?

Sid seemed to be looking at the number of each house. By the time he got to Gertrude Quinkle next door, I flung open my bedroom window, unable to stay quiet any longer.

Ignoring the gasps and camera flashes from the tourists and journalists below, I called down to him. 'Sid! I'm here!'

He looked up, but when our eyes met, I paused, feeling uncertain. I'd trusted him, but he'd encouraged me to sow the Surprising Seeds, which had ruined my life. On the other hand, I was still somehow pleased to see him.

He seemed to sense my hesitation, and gave me a tentative smile.

'I've brought food,' he said.

'I'm coming down.'

*

At the front door, Sid took one look at the wilting, crispy flowers on my head and the graffiti on the front door and sighed. 'Oh dear,' he said softly. 'This is worse than I thought.'

I bit my lip and nodded, unsure whether to invite him in or not.

He went quiet, his flecked eyes thoughtful. 'Listen, I don't want to overstay my welcome. I just wanted to bring you some food and check you're all right. There are potatoes in there from my allotment, green beans and beetroot, plus bread, cheese, milk, teabags and chocolate biscuits.' He put a bursting canvas bag at my feet.

'Thanks,' I mumbled, touched.

'Also, I found this the other day,' he said. 'And even though I know she's not your favourite person in the world right now, I thought you should have it.' He handed over a small envelope, which I tucked into my jeans pocket.

Florence licked my hand.

Sid gave me an even look. 'You know, the first time you walked into Strangeways, I thought you were one of the bravest people I'd ever met. You stood up to me when I was ranting and raving.'

'Only because I wanted to win a competition,' I grumbled.

'The point is, you stood firm. A lot of people don't

know how to, but you did. And I'll tell you another thing. Even in the depths of winter, when a garden looks as good as dead, it's actually just getting ready for spring. Sometimes, when you think everything's over, the life growing just under the surface will peek out and surprise everyone. Perhaps a new life is growing for you?'

I peered past him at the mob outside. Five tourists were standing on each other's shoulders, trying to peer into my house. On the pavement, a journalist was jabbing a big furry sound mic near our heads, trying to catch what we were saying to each other.

'Yeah,' I said slowly. *A new life as a tourist attraction and social pariah, trapped in Misery Cottage for the rest of my life. Brilliant. Just what the doctor ordered.*

'Thanks for the food,' I said more enthusiastically. 'We were peckish.'

Sid swatted away the mic and then took a deep breath. 'I've been thinking about you and the Surprising Seeds.'

My gaze hardened. 'Oh yeah?' I said.

'There must have been at least four or five different families who lived in this house before you. Haven't you ever wondered why *they* didn't hear Agatha's voice? Why they didn't find the Surprising Seeds, but you did?'

I shrugged. 'Because I was easy to fool, and they weren't?'

Sid looked at me steadily. 'It takes someone special to hear a voice from the past,' he said. 'You need an open heart to do that. It takes someone special to see a life in something small and easily overlooked, and set it free to do its work.'

'It was a *curse*,' I snapped.

Sid touched the golden flowers shooting out from his scalp.

'That,' he said softly, 'depends on your point of view.'

I stared at him and suddenly all the tumult inside my head went a little quieter.

'I'll be seeing you,' he said, his hazel-flecked eyes kind, as he turned in the hallway. 'Oh, and thanks for these.' He pointed to his head. 'Sunflowers. My favourite.'

CHAPTER 48

ONCE I'D SHUT the door, made two cups of tea and two cheese toasties and checked that Mum had eaten hers, I sat down at the kitchen table and opened the envelope Sid had brought.

Out fell a small black-and-white photograph. It showed a young woman in a pale cotton smock, standing in a sunlit garden. One hand was resting lightly on a shovel. The other was wrapped round a small tree no bigger than a broomstick. The woman had creamy skin and laughing eyes. Her joy seemed to radiate off the photo.

I turned it over. On the back was written: *Agatha and willow sapling, Cherry Cottage, 1840.*

I stared at it, my mind racing. *That* was Potty Granny Aggie? The bringer of destruction and revenge – the woman who'd cursed an entire town – was a laughing lady who planted a tree, with her hair blowing in the wind?

Tentatively, I turned it over again. The woman with the sweet eyes looked out at me, and something that had hardened around my heart fell away.

I looked at the sapling in her arms then glanced outside at the diseased willow tree, which was waving its branches about desperately, as usual. *That was hers*. Somehow, the slender tree that Aggie had planted on a sunlit day had turned sick and ugly. Maybe because, once she'd gone, it had been unloved and ignored for the rest of its lonely life. Once, it had stood in a wild-flower meadow, with a woman who loved it for company. Now, it was practically caged in a neglected patio, with owners who grimaced whenever they saw it.

Maybe it hadn't been waving its branches to taunt me at all. Maybe there had been another reason. Maybe it had wanted something else.

Love.

I put the photo down, gazed around our kitchen and began to think. The wild emotions of the last few days seemed quieter inside my head, and it felt easier than normal to travel through my own thoughts.

I thought about the windowless toddler prison that all the children of Little Sterilis went through, year by year, like pizzas on a conveyor belt, till they were spat out at the other end into a school that kept them boxed in under a roof all day long.

I thought about Neena's protest against Mr Grittysnit and how I'd been frightened of helping her because I wanted to impress a headmaster who couldn't be bothered to learn my real name. And everyone had laughed at her, even though she'd been trying to help them.

I gazed at that picture of the woman with the dancing eyes. She'd watched her favourite river disappear as it was drained for the factories that came after her. And everyone had laughed at her too, even though she'd been trying to help them.

Maybe in their shoes I'd be angry too. And maybe they'd both been right all along.

The clock in the hallway ticked loudly, eagerly.

I got up, my breath coming in short, sharp bursts.

I grabbed my denim jacket and put my trainers on. I threw a quick glance at Mum on the sofa, staring at the wall.

'Just going out, Mum,' I said. 'I'll try to be back by midday, okay?'

'Okay,' she replied tonelessly. 'See you later.'

I pushed past the tourists and the sausage stand, and I ran and I ran and I ran.

CHAPTER 49

'WHAT DO YOU want?' asked Neena.

I gazed at my best friend's face and took a deep breath. She looked *awful*. Her skin was pasty; her eyes were red-rimmed; her head allotment was a mess. Her tomatoes were gaping and split, and the small potatoes above her ears looked mouldy.

She wasn't even wearing her usual lab coat, but a bright pink top with the words *FUTURE PRINCESS* written in sparkles. If it hadn't been for those solemn brown eyes, and the telltale scab above her eyebrow, I would have said she wasn't Neena at all.

I peered past her into the empty hallway. 'Are your parents in?'

'They're at work,' she said quietly. 'What do you want?'

'I want to say sorry. I haven't said it properly yet – those texts don't really count. I see that now.'

Neena gazed at me dully, her brown eyes giving nothing away.

I tried again. 'I feel awful for what I said the other day. I shouldn't have called you a shadow.'

She shrugged and looked at the floor. 'Whatever.'

'Neena,' I said, 'you were right. I haven't been a very good friend to you lately. It's been all about me. I was so obsessed with being good it crowded everything else out.'

She blinked, and although this time her brown eyes seemed to light up with some response, she still kept one hand on the door as if she could shut it in my face at any moment.

I looked her in the eye, took a deep breath and said, 'Mr Grittysnit *was* trying to brainwash us. He just wanted us to compete against each other in how closely we could follow his stupid rules. He never cared about what we needed. And you were right to try to save our playing field. I wish I'd signed your petition. Agatha Strangeways would have been proud of you. But not as proud –' my voice wobbled, but I carried on – 'not as proud as I am. As I am to call you my best friend – if you'll still let me be.'

She looked a bit happier, but I still had the sense something was wrong.

'Okay,' she said. 'I'd like that.'

Relief as sweet as honey flooded my veins. I stuck my foot in the doorway, just to make sure she wouldn't change her mind.

'Great! What do you want to do? Shall we go into your shed? Can I borrow a lab coat? Have you still got a spare one?'

There was a ripple of pain on her forehead, and her lips sagged like someone had pulled the plug on her face. 'Not any more.'

*

'Oh my God,' I said.

'I know,' sighed Neena.

Neena's messy, dusty, cobwebby shed had been changed completely. Her desk had been polished. The floor had been mopped. The bin had been emptied. And every single scientific bit of kit that Neena had accumulated over the years had been thrown away.

Instead of test tubes, there were rolls of different-coloured tissue paper. Instead of a poster of the periodic table, there were pictures of unicorns. Her science journals and magazines from around the world had been replaced by boxes of ribbons and sequins. The dangerous mountain of crusted-over beakers had been swept away and in its place was a plastic organiser.

'What's in there?' I gasped.

'Glitter glue and felt tips,' said Neena. 'For when I'm feeling creative.'

'Where's your framed poster of Helen Sharman?' I asked, confused. Helen Sharman is a chemist, astronaut *and* the first British citizen to go into space. Neena idolised her; that poster had been up for as long as I could remember.

Silently, she pointed at the picture above the empty desk. Where Helen Sharman had once been was now a picture of a kitten next to some cupcakes with the words *KEEP CALM AND HAVE A TEA PARTY*.

'Blimey,' I said.

'I know,' said Neena. 'They bought me a whole new wardrobe too.' She plucked in dismay at her *FUTURE PRINCESS* T-shirt, as if it was bringing her out in a rash. 'And Dad wants to wallpaper the shed tomorrow. He picked out a print of elephants wearing sparkly tutus.'

'But – w-why?' I stammered in confusion.

She gave me a bleak grin. 'Well, once our story went in the papers and they found out I was partially responsible for Scalp Sprout, Mum and Dad hit the roof. They said enough was enough. They said being a scientist had literally gone to my head, and now it was time for me to knuckle down and behave like a normal young girl. Then, when Mr Grittysnit phoned them and told them I'd been petitioning against the exam hall, they really lost it.'

I hung my head in shame. She gave me a look that was kind but cross at the same time, something I thought only Mum could do.

'They said it wasn't my place to challenge authority. So they took all my stuff to the skip, and . . .' her voice trailed off, then she held her head high, 'here we are. They've had me découpaging toilet rolls for three days.' Her face revealed a world of pain. 'It's all about keeping my hands busy, apparently. They think if they throw enough sparkly glittery things my way, I'll forget all about science eventually.' Her face was ashen. No wonder her vegetables looked rotten. She was in a bad place.

My mind swam. 'Oh, Neena, I'm so sorry. This is all my fault. If I hadn't found those Seeds . . . If I hadn't dragged you along to Strangeways—'

'No!' she interrupted me with a small glimmer of her usual passion. 'Don't say that. I don't regret it for a second. It's awful I lost all my science kit and my lab, but watching the Surprising Seeds grow and spread was the most exciting experiment of my life. It was incredible to see those things at work. Everything – even this –' she gestured towards her T-shirt – 'was worth it. I'm *proud* I was part of Agatha Strangeways's revenge.'

We stared at each other for a while, and then I stepped forward and gave her the biggest, tightest hug ever.

We were quiet for a minute, in the strange shed of pointless crafts, and then a thought occurred to me. I pulled back.

'Have you still got your notebook? The one in which you wrote up our experiment?'

'Yep, I hid it under my bed as soon as I got expelled. Why?'

'It's about time I read it, don't you think?'

CHAPTER 50

SOMETIME LATER, I put the notebook down and stared at Neena in awe.

'I don't understand any of this,' I said. 'Do you mind breaking it down into English?'

She grinned. 'Okay. Well, I was convinced that the answer to the power of the Surprising Seeds lay in the soil. When Sid told us about Little Cherrybliss, he said people used to say the land here was magic. I had a hunch there must be something *different* about the soil – but what? I knew I'd have to test it somehow. So that day we sprouted, when you ran off and I stayed behind with Sid, my research began. I had a theory, you see.'

'Did you? What?' I asked.

'Well, if the garden centre has been there since Granny Aggie's time, and if all her descendants kept it safe from the Valentini family, then the earth there must be the same type of soil as it was in Aggie's day.'

'You're a genius,' I declared.

She tilted her head modestly. 'I dug some soil up from a muddy patch in the courtyard. Then I got the bus to Poorcrumble and dug some soil up from there too.'

'Why?'

'I needed a control sample – something to compare it to.'

I looked back down at the page I'd been reading. I read the sentence in front of me. *I spent night after night poring over my microscope, and after a mere twenty-five hours of testing, I'd discovered something extremely interesting about the Cherrybliss soil.*

I looked up.

Neena gave me an excited nod.

I read on. *Although the soil sample contained average levels of nitrogen, humus and phosphorous potassium compared to the test soil, it had an extra ingredient. Something that has never been found in any other soil before.*

I looked up again.

Neena had gone very still as she watched me. 'Go on,' she urged.

I scanned through the pages, skipping out the stuff I didn't fully understand. *Independent variable . . .*

hypothesis . . . blood sample taken willingly from the last living descendant . . . There was a picture of Sid, smiling gently at the camera. *Map reference . . . results . . .*

On the final page was one simple word. CONCLUSION. Underneath that, in her messy scrawl, Neena had written: *The soil sample taken from the original Cherrybliss soil contained traces of oxytocin.*

I looked at her, frowning. 'What's that?'

Neena took a deep breath. 'Oxytocin,' she said, 'is something that humans have in their bodies. Parents feel it when they look at their babies. Friends feel it when they hug. It's quite powerful stuff. It's also known as the love hormone.'

I could tell she was getting at something huge, but my tired brain limped around behind her, begging to be allowed to stop for a rest and some slices of orange.

'So?' I said finally.

'There's love inside the soil. Proper, traceable, quantifiable love. Somehow, the Strangeways were able to pass this oxytocin into the land around them, which made everything grow faster, stronger and better than anywhere else.'

'But how did this ossy— ozzy—'

'Oxytocin?'

'That's the one. How did it actually get into the soil?'

'Through the Strangeways themselves. They passed it into the soil with their own skin. Amazing, isn't it? Every time they dug up some veg or planted flowers or played in the field, somehow the love they had for the earth around them travelled from their skin into the land.'

I stared at her, feeling as if she was telling me something so big I couldn't fully understand it.

She nodded slightly, as if she guessed I felt overwhelmed. 'I even got Sid to touch some of the soil from Poorcrumble, just to test my theory. And here's the mad thing, Sorrel. When I re-examined the Poorcrumble soil after he'd touched it, I found a tiny trace of oxytocin in there. He'd changed the chemical component of the world itself just by touching it! His emotions literally went into the soil!'

I felt my heart hammering in my chest. Everything went very quiet.

'So,' said Neena slowly, as if she could tell I needed a moment to calm down. 'Sid told me that, according to Strangeways legend, Agatha buried the Seeds in 1904, when she was ninety. Which means they were buried in Cherrybliss earth under your patio for a hundred and fifteen years. The sense of betrayal that Aggie must have passed into her Seeds would have grown stronger and stronger with every year. And when you brought the Seeds and Aggie's trowel together in this shed that somehow unlocked their power.'

Neena stared at the kitten on the wall and said very quietly, 'That's about all of it.'

I stared at her. 'Neena, your research – this experiment . . . are you saying that whatever we feel about the land around us will actually go into the earth?'

'Not us. Not yet. Just the Strangeways so far. I tested myself, and when I touched several different samples, they remained unchanged. No oxytocin at all.'

'Oh,' I said, disappointed.

She grinned. 'But that's not to say it can't happen again. If generations of Strangeways folk could do it before, I think it can be done again. I just think we're all going to have to practise very, very hard.'

'But – how did Agatha actually *make* the Seeds sprout on our heads?'

Neena grinned. 'Not a clue. She's totally stumped me on that one.'

We looked at each other.

Outside, a pigeon cooed softly.

Suddenly, I remembered Mum. I didn't feel happy leaving her alone for too long with the journalists outside, goading her.

'Come on,' I said, grabbing Neena's hand.

'Where are we going?'

'Home. I have to check on Mum.'

Neena ran a hand through the rotten tomatoes flopping about on her scalp, then glanced down at her T-shirt. 'Give me a minute to get changed. There's no way I'm leaving the house in *this*.'

CHAPTER 51

ON THE WAY home, I'd warned Neena about the crowds outside Cheery Cottage. 'Just keep your head down and run through it.'

But when we got to the beginning of my road there was nothing to run through. Everybody had gone. The sausage stand, the Scalp Sprout tour guide, the Nathan Bites Fan Club – vanished. All that remained were a few tyre tracks and lots of empty coffee cups. I should have been relieved, but instead a shiver of foreboding ran down my spine.

Just as I was about to turn the key in the front door, I spotted the teenager in the black hoodie, fiddling with a bike chain round a lamp post.

'Where is everyone?' I shouted.

He whipped round and raised an eyebrow when he saw me. 'Oh, *now* you're talking?'

'Where have they gone?' I asked again. It suddenly seemed very important that we know.

He shrugged and mounted his bike. 'Back to Grittysnit School,' he said, pushing off.

'Why?' I asked, confused.

'Apparently somebody's found a cure for Scalp Sprout,' he shouted over his shoulder. 'It's waiting for them there, allegedly. Everyone's gone to cover the story.' Then he was off.

Neena and I looked at each other.

'A cure?' she said, sounding disappointed.

'Wait here – I'll get Mum,' I said.

I opened the front door, ran into the lounge and shook Mum awake.

'Geroff,' she said sluggishly. Her tree drooped despondently round her head.

I shook her again.

'Wake up, Mum,' I urged. 'Somebody's found a cure!'

This had the effect I'd been hoping for. She jumped off the sofa, eyes shining.

'Found a cure?' She gasped. 'An actual cure? How wonderful! We can get our normal life back. And I can have my hair back! Maybe I can persuade Mrs Grindstone to let me back into Chillz – I can put up with it for another few years. It pays the bills, and there's nothing wrong with that . . .'

Mum flew upstairs to get changed.

*

Five minutes later, the three of us walked down the underpass towards the school gates.

Where there had once been crowds of sobbing children and perturbed parents was now a festival atmosphere. Kids and grown-ups were milling about eagerly, wreathed in smiles. Some were giving autographs to the tourists and posing for the photographers. Everybody was laughing, pushing about impatiently, and everywhere I heard people whispering, 'A cure! A cure!'

They were so keyed up, even their dirty looks in our direction were tinged with excitement. The three of us walked around the concrete yard, and then I saw it.

A massive makeshift wooden stage next to the new exam hall. Above the stage was a banner which announced in great bold letters:

ARE YOU AFFLICTED BY SCALP SPROUT?
SICK OF BEING STARED AT?
WANT TO LOOK NORMAL AGAIN?

LINE UP HERE FOR A DOSE OF GROW-NO-MORE.

(Patent pending.)

Underneath, in smaller writing, it said:

ONLY £10 PER PERSON

CONDITIONS APPLY

Underneath *that*, in even smaller writing, it said:

SIDE EFFECTS ARE PERMANENT AND MIGHT BE UNCOMFORTABLE.

And underneath *that*, in even smaller writing still, it said:

NO REFUNDS

Next to the wooden stage was a big concrete mixer.

CHAPTER 52

PEOPLE BEGAN TO gather in front of the stage. They were craning their necks, wondering who the saviour was who'd brought the magic cure that would turn everybody back to normal again. The three of us were jostled into the middle of the throng.

'This feels weird,' Neena murmured.

I knew what she meant. But then again, wasn't this the miracle we'd all been praying for? Aggie had meant for Scalp Sprout to be a revenge, so shouldn't I be as thrilled as everybody else that things would go back to how they'd always been?

Around us, people began to shift and move about restlessly. A few started sniffing and moaning in pain. Next to me a grown man fainted right on to the ground. All of which could only mean one thing. *Chrissie is here.*

My sense of foreboding got stronger. A few seconds later, she walked on to the stage in a formal blue dress, with a matching blue turban wrapped tightly round her head. Following her was Mr Grittysnit, picking worms out of his nostrils. Chrissie's father brought up the rear.

Next to me, Mum squeezed my hand. 'I wonder what the remedy is, love,' she whispered. 'I can't wait for all this to go away, can you? You can go back to school; I'll go back to work . . . Things weren't so bad before, were they? Better the devil you know, and all that. And you'll be able to eat those Rejects again.'

I gulped down my nausea. I would never eat one of those pizzas again. They were made by a bunch of machines Mum hated. And now she was about to go right back to them with a headful of broken dreams.

On the stage, Chrissie cleared her throat. 'Ladies and gentlemen, boys and girls,' she announced, 'this has been the worst of times, no doubt about it.'

'No doubt about it,' echoed Bella.

'We've been mocked. We've been laughed at. We're the freaks of the nation. We've lost our minds, we've lost our hair, and we've lost our dignity.'

'Get a move on, darling,' said Chrissie's father, strutting about behind her. There was something a bit odd about his face. When he spoke, his mouth moved but nothing else did. His forehead was all squashed down and he looked curiously expressionless, as if he couldn't move the muscles on his face very well.

'Ladies and gentlemen, fear no more,' said Chrissie. 'Cry no more. Grow no more. Allow me to introduce the man behind Valentini Constructions and the saviour of the day. My father, Rufus Valentini!'

The crowd burst into rapturous applause.

Chrissie's father took centre stage. He tried to smile but the hat on his head was so tight that the corners of his mouth merely twitched.

'Let's get down to brass tacks here. This disease has been a nightmare, am I right?'

A groan of assent rippled through the crowd.

'I know you've all been in despair about this Scalp Sprout. And nothing seems to get rid of it. The doctors don't know what to do. The school doesn't know what to do. Heck, even you don't know what to do, am I right?'

In front of me, a host of wilted flowers and plants bobbed up and down and rustled sadly.

'But I've got the one thing that will stop this Scalp Sprout for ever.'

The crowd gasped.

'Tell us, tell us!' shouted somebody.

Mr Valentini proudly gestured to the concrete mixer beside him. He nodded to the man in a fluorescent jacket standing by it. The man flipped a switch and, with a deafening whir and a clang, the mixer came to life and started churning in circles. Mr Valentini looked at his machine as tenderly as if it was his firstborn, and then he turned back to us.

'Water, aggregate, cement,' he said lovingly.

'Eh?' said somebody in the crowd.

'Mix it all together, and you get concrete,' said Mr Valentini. 'Lovely, solid, heavy, nature-hating concrete; nothing gets past that baby. If you want to get rid of your Scalp Sprout, concrete is the solution. Tried it myself,' he said, pointing at his head. 'And as you can see, not one single green thing survived.'

So it wasn't a hat – Mr Valentini had poured his own concrete on his head. That explained why he looked so squashed and hot and curiously lifeless.

'My family and I have been pouring tonnes and tonnes of concrete on land over the last century or so,' he said. 'Made a pretty penny, I can tell you! And without a doubt, ladies and gentlemen, this is the cure you've all been waiting for!'

'How do we use it?' somebody shouted.

'I'll pour it on, straight from the cement mixer, with the aid of this little funnel here,' he announced grandly, holding up a simple plastic cone. 'Then all you have to do is let it set.'

Mr Valentini, Chrissie and Mr Grittysnit stared out at the crowd smugly.

'Right then, who's going to go first?' asked Mr Grittysnit.

The horde around me buzzed with anticipation and a sea of hands shot up. Then, as the concrete mixer seemed to get even louder, a few hands slunk nervously back down.

'After you,' people started saying.

'No, no, I insist,' others said. 'After *you*.'

Mr Valentini tutted in frustration. 'Come on, come on,' he urged. 'I haven't got all day. I've got a community garden to bulldoze in the next town by four.'

A shy voice from the back of the crowd said, 'I'll go first.'

'Aha!' said Mr Valentini. 'Our first client! Make way for the lad. Let's be seeing you. No need to be sad any more, dear fellow.'

As people parted and the speaker got closer to the stage, I saw with a shock that it was Bertie. He did look a sorry sight. Underneath the hectic blush on his cheeks, his skin was waxy pale, and the wallflowers on his head were so brown and crisp they looked like a bunch of twigs. Bertie walked up the steps to the wooden stage and stood, looking out, scratching his face nervously.

'Do you hate what you've become, boy?' barked Mr Valentini.

Bertie nodded, and the two men smiled approvingly. It was a terrifying sight.

'Think your head's ridiculous, boy?'

Bertie nodded again.

'Ashamed to be seen with those flowers, eh? What you want is a nice solid hat of concrete – much manlier, eh? Maybe this will be the making of you,' said Mr Valentini. 'Sit here, boy.'

He pointed to a stool on the stage and Bertie sat on it. It was like watching somebody get ready for their own execution; I half expected Bertie to say his final words. But Bertie said nothing and merely stared at the ground, his cheeks aflame.

At a nod from Mr Valentini, the man in the fluorescent jacket and a hard hat moved the cement mixer closer to Bertie, who had closed his eyes and was swallowing nervously. The whir and the clang and the scrape of the concrete inside the mixer got louder. Then it tipped forward so we could all see the thick, grey sludge pulsing inside.

A few people began to clap.

Within seconds it would be all over Bertie's head, and he would look just like Mr Valentini. Grey on the top, and squished underneath.

I took a deep breath and caught the faintest trace of the sprouting heads around me as they lived their final minutes; a sweet, smoky tang of flowers and plants and ferns and things growing and living.

My mind raced. I saw in my mind's eye the woman with laughing eyes, planting something she'd loved in a meadow. Something which had then been ignored, unloved and smothered in concrete so it could never grow properly again.

SCRICK, SCRICK.

CHAPTER 53

WITH THE PRECISION of a brain surgeon, Mr Valentini carefully positioned the funnel on top of Bertie's head. 'Nearly there, boy,' he barked.

Bertie looked up miserably and gave a tentative smile.

A thick oozy stream of concrete began its descent down the funnel towards his head.

Strange and unsettling memories of the past week began to whip around inside me, like I was being spun round a carousel called My Life.

SPIN!

Mum's bitten fingernails.

SPIN!

May conformity mould you.

SPIN!

'You should be sorry, Sorry.'

SPIN!

'It was countryside, green and wild . . .'

My skin prickled. Perhaps going back to normal *wasn't* what we needed. Perhaps normality was hugely overrated. And perhaps the terrible things that had been done to Little Cherrybliss weren't ancient history – maybe it was *still* happening. Julius Valentini stole a green world from Aggie and our entire town had been shaped by that theft.

And every day we did nothing about it, we were robbed a little more.

My heart beat faster. What was it Neena had said to me once? *'The fight's only over when you think it's over.'*

Somebody in the crowd shouted 'STOP!'

Mum and Neena were staring at me, looking surprised, and I realised it was me doing the shouting.

I said it again, just to be sure. 'STOP!'

I let go of Mum's hand. I pushed my way through the crowd and ran up the steps on to the stage, past a furiously spluttering Mr Valentini. I hurried to the concrete mixer and, without even thinking what I was doing, I flicked the switch off. With a groan and a protesting *whir* and *fluump*, the concrete mixer went silent and the funnel dropped down, narrowly missing Bertie.

There was a deathly silence behind me and I turned round to face the crowd.

'It's her! It's the girl who's done all of this,' shouted a cross woman with a headful of spiky cacti.

People hissed and booed.

'You should be ashamed of yourself,' shouted somebody.

I stared out at a sea of angry faces and wilted heads and saw Nathan Bites smirking back at me. I gulped. What was I meant to do now? Maybe I should have thought this through. Just a few notes on an index card would have been helpful. But the pipe in my brain which normally pumped out words seemed to have got clogged. Maybe Mum had something to unblock it? I looked at her desperately.

'Get off the stage, Sorry Fallowfield. You've no place at this school,' said Mr Grittysnit.

I locked eyes with Neena. She grinned at me and gave an encouraging nod. And that was enough.

I took a deep breath and opened my mouth. 'Actually, Mr Grittysnit, you're wrong there.'

There was an audible intake of breath.

Somebody whispered, 'The cheek!'

'I *should* be here. I'm the one responsible for what we've all grown. But first things first. I'm Sorrel. That's my name. It's not Sorry or Suck-up. Mum called me

Sorrel. So you can call me by my proper name from now on. And that goes for you too, Chrissie.'

Chrissie stared at me, her eyes wide, and I returned her gaze until she dropped hers and started looking at her shoes.

That was a first.

I took a deep breath. 'The papers were right. I made this happen.'

There were gasps in the crowd. The journalists whipped out their pens and started scribbling things down.

A gentle breeze caressed the flowers on my head, and they danced in response.

'But I didn't invent anything in Neena's shed. What *actually* happened was, I found a packet of Surprising Seeds buried in my backyard, and I sprinkled them on my head and on Neena's and Mum's. I had no control over how quickly they spread and how quickly they grew. I couldn't do anything to stop them. I know you think they've ruined your lives. I know you're tired of being gawped at by tourists and you miss your old hair and you don't like looking different. I know all of that, and for *that*, I am sorry.'

'Surprising Seeds, my foot,' someone muttered, and

a nasty laugh began to ripple through the crowd in front of me.

I have to work harder to convince them. What should I say next? Where do I start?

Perhaps I should just start with the truth.

'But you don't know everything yet. There's something the journalists *haven't* written about. And that's the woman who created the Surprising Seeds in the first place. Agatha Strangeways.'

Mr Valentini began to laugh extra loudly, as if to drown me out, and for a second I faltered. But the gentle breeze on my skin felt like someone encouraging me, so I tried again, louder this time.

'Agatha and her ancestors owned this land, a long time ago,' I said. 'Back when it was called Little Cherrybliss. It was beautiful, and wild. The people who lived here loved it. There weren't any shopping centres, bookies, car parks, plastic toy shops or windowless play centres. There were meadows and woods and a river for kids to swim in.'

'Rubbish!' said a voice in the crowd.

'And why should we care?' shouted someone else. 'What's wrong with shopping and parking anyway?'

The tuts and boos grew louder, and Mr Valentini's

horrible fake laugh did too, as if he was encouraging the jeers. My cheeks burned. I wasn't getting through to them. I was embarrassing myself, and Mum. *Perhaps I should just go.*

I glanced at the steps leading off the stage and at that exact moment, the breeze got a tiny bit stronger. I felt it stroke my legs and it gave me a peculiar strength. My voice came out shaky but loud.

'We *should* care about what happened to the river and the wood and the meadow, because they were *stolen* from us. And if we don't care then people will *keep* taking things away from us – like space to play in and nature – that we deserve to have. And then we won't even need to bother standing under that funnel; we'll already be smothered.'

Mr Valentini, who clearly didn't like not being the centre of attention and whose snorts of contemptuous laughter had been getting progressively louder, nudged me sharply with one elbow, as if he wanted to push me out of the way.

'Smothered? Suprising Seeds? Pull the other one! You're not making any sense, sweetheart. It all sounds like a silly fairy tale made up by a little girl who should know better,' he sneered. 'Goodness me, some people will do anything to stay in the limelight, won't they? But never mind, moving swiftly on, let's get back to making things right—'

'Yeah, funny you should say that, Mr Valentini,' I heard myself saying in a shaky voice. 'About making things right. Because your family poisoned land to take it from a woman who loved it. So if *anyone* needs to make up for that, I guess it's you.'

Mr Valentini gave a tiny gulp that I doubt anyone from the crowd would have noticed, but it gave me enough courage to keep talking.

'That's right, isn't it? And the Valentini family haven't stopped poisoning Little Cherrybliss since—'

'LIAR!' It was Chrissie, her cheeks aflame. By the stunned, horrified look on her face I realised she hadn't got to that part in Neena's notebook. 'How dare you say that about my family? How dare you?' Her voice wobbled. She looked up at her father, and she suddenly looked much younger than normal. 'She's lying, isn't she, Daddy? We never really did that, did we? Tell her, Daddy – tell her she's lying.'

In the tiny fraction of the second that it took for Mr Valentini to look her in the eye, something seemed to come over Chrissie that made her shoulders slump.

The crowd was completely silent.

'Listen, sweetheart,' he said in the tone of an exasperated nursery teacher, 'this was all a *long* time ago. There comes a certain time when you need to –' he shot me a loaded look – '*get over things*. Besides, it was business.' He lifted his chin, as if he was pleased that this family secret was finally out in the open. 'All's fair when it comes to moneymaking – isn't that what Mummy and Daddy have always said? You certainly wouldn't have your ponies and your helicopter if old Julius hadn't begun our family fortune, and that's a cold hard fact.'

Chrissie just stared at the ground.

This seemed to satisfy Mr Valentini, who, his confidence restored, bared his teeth in a grin that reminded me of Sid's secateurs glinting in the sunlight. 'Shall we crack on?'

From the eager nods in front of us, I realised that most of the people in our town didn't care about what had happened to Little Cherrybliss. How can you feel sad about losing something if you never had it to begin with?

As if they could sense that I'd finally run out of steam, some of the adults in the crowd began to do a horrible, slow clap.

'Off!' someone shouted. 'Off!'

'Wait,' I heard a little boy say. 'I want to hear the rest of her story—'

But his voice was drowned out by others picking up the chant. 'SORREL – OFF. CEMENT MIXER – ON.'

Behind me, the concrete mixer clanged into life once more.

And the gentle breeze suddenly gained strength.

CHAPTER 54

THE WIND SCREAMED across the tarmac.

It took what it wanted from the crowd, whistling as it went. Petals, leaves and crumbs of soil flew out of our heads, through the air and into the eye of what had now become a whirling spiral, circling and moving through the crowd.

As we watched, these scraps whipped themselves into the shape of something undeniably human. As it fluttered across the concrete yard, it began to resemble a slender, light-footed woman. I felt that looking at it head-on could be dangerous, like staring straight at the sun, yet I couldn't help stealing a tiny glance. And for a second, the rippling flurry of leaves and soil seemed to arrange themselves into the faintest impression of a face. I glimpsed a pair of blazing eyes and a smile that was hard to read, before they too spun and whirled and became part of the cyclone of flowers and earth winding around each other.

And I knew that we were in the presence of Agatha Strangeways somehow, yet she was also mixed up with something else. She was human and more than human; she had become part of the land that she had so loved.

The land we hadn't treated very nicely since she'd gone.

What could possibly go wrong? How lovely you could make it!

Her appearance silenced us completely. Speech seemed impossible. Mr Valentini and Mr Grittysnit had turned white. All we could do was stare as Agatha walked through the crowd, nature churning inside her like a desperate dog locked up for too long.

Slowly, her shimmering shape began to mount the steps of the stage.

My entire body trembled. She plainly wasn't done with us yet.

What if she made some kind of hideous creeping ivy sprout out of our heads and pour into our mouths and twist round our essential inner organ-y bits, binding us all in a clammy growing net in which we would suffocate to death?

Not that I wanted to give her any ideas.

Too late for that, I'm afraid, said her raspy voice

inside my head. ***Don't forget, we're bound together, us two. I can peep into your brain from time to time – you might want to remember that.***

You're not actually going to make a creeping ivy suffocate us, are you?

Quiet while I think, child. This is all a bit of a spur-of-the-moment thing – I haven't fully thought it out yet.

Okay, but if you want some hints on who to start with, how about that man over there in the tight suit?

That's enough from you. I'm an awesome life force – let me work.

Agatha shifted and faced the crowd, which gasped and stared and gulped. Cameras flashed. Children shrieked.

I know what you're thinking. Why didn't we make a run for it? But we couldn't. We were rooted to the spot – fear for your life has a way of doing that. Plus we'd never seen anything like her before. All we could do was stare.

I searched the crowd frantically, desperate for one last glimpse of Mum's face before our final judgement.

'I'm sorry,' I mouthed.

She shook her head and whispered something

back, but the wind stole her words away.

Then Agatha lifted her fluttering arms to cast her final retribution, and I bowed my head. This was it. We hadn't repented, we hadn't changed enough, and now we were going to pay the price. She was probably going to turn us all into trees; our feet would become twisted, gnarly roots that would burrow into the ground and we would be stuck there for ever, a forest of doomed humans.

That's another excellent idea, Sorrel. You could sell these to other vengeful spirits – I can put you in touch with a few I know.

Thanks, that's very comforting.

I'm not sure I like your tone.

Agatha held her palms up to the sky.

And then the weirdest thing happened.

Instead of dying or turning into a Brussels sprout, I felt everything inside my head start to glow. The birdsong in the trees grew louder, and it filled my head like a huge glittering wave that broke over my thoughts and washed everything away. My shoulders relaxed. The tight threads of anxiety which had been pulling at my insides were cut loose instantly.

I breathed out. I breathed in. The air filling my body

felt like tiny crystals of the purest oxygen, sweeter and cleaner than anything I had ever tasted.

I breathed out. I breathed in. Those waves moved up and down against the shores of my mind. I felt as if I belonged to the world, and it, in turn, was part of me.

What am I feeling? I asked her.

It's too big for a name.

It's a bit overwhelming.

It can be, at first.

By the stunned faces in front of me, I realised everyone else was feeling it too. Could this be the oxy-thingy Neena had told me about? Was this all the love that the Strangeways had poured into their land, year after year? Had Agatha somehow brought it with her, and made it flow back into us?

Just when I began to think that perhaps she wasn't as scary as she looked and we'd got her all wrong, she turned towards Mr Valentini.

CHAPTER 55

INSTANTLY HIS BLUSTER left him. His mouth shook, his shoulders trembled and he sank to his knees with his hands held out in front of him.

'I'm sorry,' he said through quivering lips. 'Please don't hurt me.'

But the beautiful fluttering shape beside me gave a terrible grin.

At the look of terror on Chrissie's face, I reached out an arm to stop Agatha. But I was too late. She lifted her hands and the air in front of us flexed and bent.

There was an awful sound of something cracking open.

Mr Valentini shrieked with pain and reached upwards, and the crowd moaned. But when he pulled his hands away, we saw that it was not his skull that had been shattered, but the cement on his head, which was now landing on the ground around him in bits. Out of his head tumbled hundreds of sky-blue flowers on long green tendrils.

'Forget-me-not,' Agatha said.

Mr Valentini looked like a confused schoolboy as he touched a lock of his new hair.

'Forget *me* not,' said Agatha again.

This time he looked up into her face. 'I won't forget,' he mumbled.

'Make things right,' insisted Agatha.

He nodded, and the two of them stared at each other for a long time.

A deep sigh escaped Agatha, the sort which hurts, like something painful has been released.

She squeezed my hand.

You heard the man, she said.

I heard the man.

It's time for me to go. You're in charge now.

I squeezed Agatha's hand back, and the leaves and the flowers and the crumbs of soil came apart, and she was gone, yet I felt a trace of that feeling inside me still. Compared to its earlier intensity, it was now just the faintest echo of the wild green force she'd become. Even so, it was enough. Like a lighthouse, her beam had caught us in its sweep; she'd blazed so brightly that now a gleam of her wildness shone inside us too. You only had to look around to know it.

We regarded each other in the soft afternoon light as if seeing each other for the first time.

Chrissie walked over to the concrete mixer and turned it off. Then she cleared her throat and looked at me levelly.

'Chrissie—' began her father.

'Shut up, Daddy.' She turned to me. 'Tell us everything,' she said firmly. 'From the beginning.'

So I did.

CHAPTER 56

Sometime later, Mum, Sid, Miss Mossheart, Chrissie, Neena and I stood in the backyard of Cheery Cottage. With us was a huge pneumatic drill, a lorry-load of garden supplies we'd picked up from Strangeways, the entire Valentini Constructions crew and most of the Laminator class. It was quite a tight squeeze.

'Right then,' said the foreman. 'Fire her up.'

The pneumatic drill roared into life. For the second time in my life I watched as the concrete in our backyard broke and split apart, and this time it made me glad. As each slab was shattered and lifted off, revealing rich, dark brown earth underneath, we all cheered. The sun turned fat and orange in the late-afternoon sky as we carried the concrete out of the yard and chucked it into the skip outside our house.

Eventually, there were just four slabs left to prise off. The ones round the base of the willow tree.

I walked over and placed my hand on its rough

red bark. 'All that time, I thought you were trying to scare me. But you weren't, were you? You just wanted a friend.'

Its leaves rustled in the wind in reply, and I felt a fierce and sudden love rush out of my hand and into the bark. The drill roared into life once more, and when the last of the slabs had been thrown into the skip, Chrissie nudged me, smiling. 'Look,' she said.

I looked.

At the top of the willow tree was a radiant green light. As it swept down the trunk, it washed away the red carbuncles, painful-looking rash, black mildew spots and sores. Its withered branches and leaves swelled and grew with life. The beautiful green willow tree stood proudly against the glowing sky.

And something else changed too. In front of our eyes, Chrissie's purple corpse flower disappeared and was replaced by a headful of creamy roses.

I'm not a total *witch*, said Aggie's voice softly inside my head.

On the brown earth, we sprinkled grass seed. Then we brought out loads of beautiful, colourful shrubs, plants and flowers that we'd chosen at Strangeways.

As we put them into the rich, crumbly soil, Sid

named each one. 'Sweet peas, celandine, cornflowers, purple asters and ox-eye daisies. Roses, hellebores, sweet violets, delphiniums, lady's mantle . . .'

I turned round and stared at my home. Even from the outside, it looked different – brighter and lighter. Somehow, I knew that the kitchen tap wouldn't be dripping sadly any more.

I gulped down a mug of tea, faced my friends and grinned. 'Where shall we smash up next?'

ONE YEAR ON

I TWISTED MY key in the lock and walked into the empty house. On sore feet, I trudged into the kitchen and, sighing with tiredness, peeled off my overalls before chucking them in the washing machine. I mopped the marmalade off the counter, threw the teabags away and glanced at the note on the fridge to check Mum's work shift.

Then I went upstairs, put on my swimsuit under my leggings and T-shirt, and went out into our back garden. I lay on my back on the soft green grass and gazed up into the rustling leaves of the willow tree, pondering the busy morning I'd had at Strangeways in my new Saturday job.

As assistant gardener, I now spent most of my weekends down at Strangeways. We were very busy; demand for plants, shrubs, flowers and seeds had suddenly shot up. When we weren't serving at the till or checking on the seedlings in the new greenhouses, we were running lessons and workshops to help people learn how to grow for themselves, as well as care for their own heads.

There were always quite a few tourists to meet too, which was okay, as they were happy to donate to our Plants for Everywhere stall in return for some selfies.

In fact, Strangeways was so busy now that Sid was thinking of taking on more assistants. I had about three children in mind, all of whom had been coming to the Get to Know Your Plants Sunday school sessions for six months now, which took place in the spruced-up courtyard, under the photo of Aggie and her willow-tree sapling which we'd framed and hung up on a wall.

I stretched happily on the soft grass. Today felt like a day for celebrating. I'd recently finished writing up my account of what had really happened in my town. And there was a nice publishing company in London who said they would turn it into a book, so everyone would know the truth about the Surprising Seeds, once and for all.

My thoughts were interrupted by the sound of my mobile beeping with a text from Neena. *Just finishing up in the lab. Meet you at the café? N x*

I sent a reply. *See you there in half an hour x*

Neena had spent the past year working with scientists from the London School of Science to write up and further test her results on 'Emotional Osmosis between Humans and Soil, Using the Strangeways Family as Evidence'. They've been so impressed with her research, she's been offered a place there when she turns eighteen. Her famous yellow notebook has been printed in every medical journal around the world.

She donated all her crafty stuff to the new art department at our school. Bertie's in charge of it, mostly.

Bertie has moved on from his snake series, which would come as a relief to Mr Grittysnit, if we only knew where he was.

Last I heard, he was holed up in a hospital in Bulgaria, with special worm-pulling experts working round the clock on his nostrils. I expect Granny Aggie will get tired of the joke eventually and put him out of his misery . . . one day.

The poster of the kitten staring at the cupcakes now hangs on the wall at our mums' outdoor café.

Neena's dad never wallpapered the shed.

I grabbed my bag and hopped on my brand-new

racing bike, pausing on the high street to stop and say hello to Chrissie.

'How's it going?' I asked.

'On schedule.' Chrissie grinned, clutching a sheaf of architectural plans.

'Is it time for a tea break yet, love?' shouted the wiry, muscled man in the hard hat from the highest beam of scaffolding above her.

'Not yet, Dad,' said Chrissie. 'Put in a few more hours first.'

'Fair enough,' Mr Valentini said, wiping the sweat off his brow with a handkerchief.

As the banging of his hammer recommenced, she shot me a grin. 'See you at the river?'

'See you at the river,' I replied, and went on my way.

Mr Valentini had more than fulfilled his promise to make things right, I reflected as I cycled down the high street, admiring his work on the buildings that I passed. He now ran a new company, Roofless Deconstruction, which specialised in installing roofs that slid back on buildings. And he did them all for free.

All the offices, shops, and both Chillz and the dishcloth factory had them now. All of the grown-ups looked so much happier – and less pale.

He'd also installed a sliding-back roof on our new school, the Agatha Strangeways Academy. We use it on sunny days, so everyone can top up the sunlight on their heads while they learn.

To be honest, we usually slide it back on overcast days too.

And windy days.

And rainy days . . .

Okay, yep, it's almost always open.

Our new headmistress, Miss Mossheart, is very strict – about making sure we grow properly. At the slightest look of a crispy flower, wilting fern or mouldy vegetable, we get sent along to our new communal greenhouse that got built over the original exam hall site. It's really nice – there are hammocks and someone rigged up watering stations, so we can chill, read our books in sunny spots and give our heads a drink.

In her spare time, Miss Mossheart heads up the Little Cherrybliss Restoration Squad, run by volunteers. Everyone in the town gets stuck in. Over the last year, thanks to a very generous anonymous donation of cash (delivered by a forklift truck) and lots of elbow grease, we've transformed the place.

I cycled on for a few miles, past the wild-flower

meadows, lavender fields, communal allotments, and through the newly planted woods that now encircled Little Cherrybliss. Neena was waiting for me by the outdoor café in the nature reserve. After we'd said hi to its famously cheerful chefs – our mums – and waited in line with what felt like the rest of the town to buy their bestselling brownies and lemonade, we slowly made our way to the grassy banks of the newly restored Cherrybliss river, which now bubbled and gurgled its way through the entire town.

The sunlight sparkled on the water.

I brushed a lock of fragrant flowers away from my forehead. Bit into my brownie. Thought about how nice a swim would feel after a morning in the sunshine.

'There was a tiny accident this week at the printer,' I said conversationally, after the last delicious crumb had been wiped off my plate.

'Oh yeah?' said Neena, raising a newly singed eyebrow. 'What happened?'

'Well, I took my notes along, so they could get printed into loads of books about everything that happened here . . .'

'Right,' said Neena.

'But when I handed over the manuscript to the

printer, I could have sworn I saw a couple of seeds lying on top of the very first page.'

Neena looked at me sharply. 'Seeds? What did they look like?'

'Well, they were small. And black. And they had four little tendrils sticking out of them, like jellyfish.'

'Or aliens?' she asked, tilting her head and looking at me steadily.

'Yep,' I nodded, gazing up at the sky and not quite meeting her eye. 'Total accident, of course. Feel really bad about it.'

Neena cleared her throat. 'Are you saying that one of the books might have Surprising Seeds in its pages?'

I looked at my muddy fingernails. 'One,' I admitted. 'Or two.'

'So if there's a child somewhere in the country, reading the book in bed, a Surprising Seed might fall out of the pages and land on their head? And that, should the circumstances be right, there might be a new epidemic on the way?'

I nodded. 'That's exactly what I'm saying.'

Our eyes met.

'Here's hoping,' said Neena.

'Fingers crossed,' I agreed.

We gazed out at the river together in companionable silence. And, just for a second, I thought I heard the sound of an old woman chuckling softly, as the stream moved down the riverbed.

THE END

ACKNOWLEDGEMENTS

I would like to thank my very first readers, Bon, Jayden, Milly, Harry, Esme and Eliana, who said such nice things about my second draft and encouraged me to keep going; members of the South-West SCBWI for their enthusiasm and advice, especially Jan, Mike, Fran, Amanda and Nicola K; 'Warrior' Jules, Canadian John and Penny for school-run pep talks, Sally and the Gibbs Gang for letting me borrow names and providing cake fuel; my friends Vicky, Meg and Melissa for being lovely human beings; and most of all Ben, for keeping me alive, warm and fed for quite a long time.

When I was a child, my parents always made sure I had books to read and libraries to visit. Thank you, Mum, for writing me stories when you were at work and telling me spooky German fairy tales, and thank you, Dad, for your love of language. I wouldn't be a writer if it wasn't for both of you.

Agatha Strangeways took a while to make her presence felt and for that, and also for championing my story when I most needed it, I'd like to thank my agent, Silvia Molteni. And a huge thanks to my editor,

Nick Lake, and the team at HarperCollins UK for, you know, MAKING DREAMS COME TRUE.

And, Polly, you wondrous grass, snail, slug, flower, mud, stone, stick, tree and dandelion-loving child, thank you for making this book happen in so many ways. You are the best thing I ever grew.

Turn over for a sneak preview from Nicola Skinner's next brilliant book, *Storm*, about a furious person called Frances . . .

Frances's parents were not prepared for her birth: they had a blanket and an easel and some paint, but not anything useful, like a car or a phone. So it's no wonder Frankie has always had a temper. She was born on a beach, in a STORM.

But Frankie is about to discover that there are things more important than herself – and that anger has its uses. Because when you have a storm inside you – sometimes the only thing to do is let it out . . .

Poltergeist: a type of ghost or spirit responsible for loud, chaotic and destructive disturbances. A noisy ghost. From the German *poltern* (to make sound) and *geist* (ghost).

Some people think we don't exist.
They're wrong.

PART ONE

1
A BIT EGGY

When you're born, you're a baby. That's something we can all agree on. But you're not *just* a baby. No.

You're a story.

A beautiful, bouncing, gurgling story.

A tale to be treasured.

And not just one story either. You're all of the stories, all of the time. You're an adventure, a love story, a thriller, occasionally a horror – yes, I am looking at you, you naughty little scamp – all rolled into one. And every day is story time now *you've* arrived.

Basically, babies are page-turners, and will only get more fascinating with each passing day. Or that's what their parents think anyway.

Even if no one else does.

Parents *love* talking about their children, don't they? Stick around any school gate long enough and all you'll hear is: 'my treasure this' and 'my darling that'. And what do they love to talk about the *most*?

Our beginning.

Also known as *the Birth*.

This part is special.

It is sacred.

It is long.

Have a look around. Go on.

Are there parents nearby? Is their conversation turning towards childbirth? Do any of them have a funny misty-eyed look on their face? Is anyone – this is the clincher – *clearing their throat*?

If the answer to any of that is *yes*, then I ask you this. Have you got an escape route? If you have, run to it. Now.

If not, tough luck. Did you have something planned for the day? Not any more you don't. Because when a parent breaks into a birth story, it takes a while and there's nowhere to hide.

You will hear:

a. When the contractions started.

b. Which hospital they decided to drive to.

c. What song was on the radio in the car.

d. Whether that glitchy traffic light had been fixed.

Not to mention:

a. How much the parking cost.
b. Whether that was reasonable.
c. What pain relief was available.
d. And how much the baby weighed.

(This last bit captivates them all, for some mysterious reason. Like farmers and their prize-winning turnips, parents are obsessed with how much their babies weigh. Why? Who knows? Ask *them*, if you don't mind waving goodbye to another day of your life.)

Anyway, you'd better pay attention. Make sure you listen closely and nod thoughtfully in all the right places, as if you're having a fantastic time. If you don't listen hard enough, they'll somehow know, with that uncanny parental sixth sense, and *start all over again from the top*. Then it will be YOU asking for pain relief.

For your ears.

And I'll tell you another thing. For your entire life, how you were born will be used to explain you. Why you *are* how you *are*. Parents will say stuff like 'Oh, it's no wonder our Jasper is so good at ballroom dancing – after all, he was born on a Tuesday just after I'd had a ham sandwich' or 'Well, of *course* Deidre's a dawdler – she was born just shy of the M25!', and all the other parents will nod solemnly like this makes total sense, pour themselves another cup of tea, and say, 'Tell me again what she weighed'.

Mine were the same. They'd bring up the way I was born at the drop of a hat. Especially when I was cross. And they'd always say the same thing: 'Well, that's what happens when you're born in a storm.'

This, of course, would only make things worse. I mean, it's very difficult to discuss the injustice of the recycling rota when your parents just keep bringing up the weather.

From eleven years ago.

It didn't end there either. Once they started, there was no stopping them. My birth story was so well rehearsed in our house it was like a duet. My parents had their lines and they knew them well.

'You were born raging, Frances Frida Ripley.' That's how Dad would start. 'Salty from the get go, you were.' (Frances Frida Ripley is me by the way. Hi. Except I'd rather you didn't call me Frances, if that's okay. Frankie's fine.)

Then Mum would interrupt. 'Well, love, that's not

completely true. Frankie was a very peaceful baby girl. A little wet, a bit cold, perhaps, but so calm. So still. You looked as if you didn't have a care in the world.'

That would have been the hypothermia kicking in, Mum.

'Yeah, you were peaceful, for all of a second,' Dad would add. 'Right up until the moment you took your first breath.' Tiny smiles would fly between them, like birds swooping home. '*That* was when you started raging. And you haven't really stopped since.' Then, at a look from Mum, he'd mutter, 'But we wouldn't have you any other way, of course' and lope off towards his painting shed.

But here's my take on it: what did they expect? Of *course* I lost my temper when I was born. I mean, they were the ones who decided to have a baby on a freezing beach! On top of some pebbles! In the middle of winter! In a *storm*! No wonder I got a bit eggy. Any sensible baby would.

2
MY BIRTH STORY

Anyway, it wasn't my fault. It was their idea to head down to the beach that day, even though Mum was heavily pregnant with me. Even after they saw the thick black storm clouds circling our small village.

They *could* have done something sensible instead, like driving to the nearest hospital on a test run, making a careful note of how much the parking cost and whether that was reasonable. Perhaps then I would have turned into a very different child and this would be a very different story.

But they weren't practical people.

'I wanted to paint the storm,' Dad said. 'Stand inside it. See its colours.'

Dad said stuff like this regularly. He was an artist. He was nuts about colours. For his day job, he painted pet portraits. Didn't matter if they were scaly, hairy, sweet or scary, if you had £275 to splash out on a nine-inch by twelve-inch painting of your pet (unframed) then Dad, also known as Dougie Ripley – also known as

Cliffstones' One and Only
Pet Portrait Painter!

– was your man.

In his spare time, though, he painted the sea.

'I'll never get close to showing the sea the way she looks in my head,' he'd say to us – us being me and Birdie (my six-year-old sister).

'Why paint it, then?' we'd ask.

In reply he'd tap the side of his nose and smile his wonky smile. 'It's the pull of it,' he'd say then. 'You can't deny the pull of it.'

Whatever that meant.

And don't even get me started on Mum. She was practically nine months pregnant on the day of the storm. She could have sat about on the sofa complaining about her swollen ankles, like any normal pregnant woman. She *could* have said, 'No, Douglas Ripley, we are not going to the beach in the middle of a hurricane, not on your nelly. Now drive me to the nearest hospital so I can have this baby, and put the radio on because apparently that's important.'

But she didn't.

'I was sick of staring at our four walls, Frankie, and I thought the sea air would make me feel better. You weren't due for another week anyway, so you can take that look off your face for starters.'

Here's what they didn't take:

1. A phone.
2. A car.
3. Anything practical in case one of them gave birth.

Here's what they took:

a. A moth-eaten picnic blanket.
b. Mum's favourite coral lipstick.
c. Dad's easel and paints.

Anyway, unsurprisingly, Mum went into labour just after they got to the shingle beach down by the harbour. No one else was around, what with it being

January. And the storm. And having normal brains.

And without 1, 2 and 3, it finally dawned on Mum and Dad that I was going to be born right on top of a. The moth-eaten picnic blanket. So they threw it on top of some lumpy pebbles and hoped for the best. Which was completely against NHS guidelines at the time, especially under the bit called 'Good Places to Have a Baby'.

I was not swaddled in a comfy hospital blanket and cooed over by nurses. Instead I was bundled into a damp hoodie and seagulls squawked over my head. To cap it all off, I opened my mouth for some milk but got a mouthful of salt spray instead. And that was my first taste of the world: a lungful of storm.

According to Mum, it moulded me for ever. 'You changed, right then and there,' she'd say. 'I watched the storm come over you, as sudden as a fever. You clenched your tiny fist and you raged up at the sky, like you were having a competition about who could be louder.'

A coral smile would flash on her lips, quick as a fish. 'And sometimes I think a bit of that storm's been stuck inside you ever since.'

Then she'd wander off in the direction of her study,

stopping on the way to make her one billionth coffee of the day. Then, *just* as I'd begin to think I'd got away with it, she'd say, 'Oh, and don't forget to put the recycling out.'

And that was my birth story.

But here's an inescapable fact about being born. You might live until you're 101, experience wild success and mountain peaks and dancing monkeys, but however you live and whatever you do, the story of your life will end with a death.

Yours.

That's the deal. Because the thing about human stories is: they all finish more or less the same way. On the final page. *The end.*

But because you're dead you never normally hear that bit.

Normally.